JOURNEYS
WITH
STELLARMAN

FRANCIS A. ANDREW

Order this book online at www.trafford.com
or email orders@trafford.com

Most Trafford titles are also available at major online book retailers.

Printed in the United States of America.

ISBN: 978-1-4669-5137-2 (sc)
ISBN: 978-1-4669-5139-6 (hc)
ISBN: 978-1-4669-5138-9 (e)

Library of Congress Control Number: 2012914152

Trafford rev. 08/06/2012

 www.trafford.com

North America & international
toll-free: 1 888 232 4444 (USA & Canada)
phone: 250 383 6864 ♦ fax: 812 355 4082

CONTENTS

This book is dedicated to Sir Patrick Moore whose programme,
The Sky at Night, did so much to enkindle my interest in astronomy.

TOUGH ASSIGNMENT

"Wilbur Barnes! For a 12 year old boy you do like to bite off more than you are capable of chewing."

"But Miss Stricto, I'm very interested in astronomy."

"Well, you've chosen your assignment and you'll have to stick to it. And don't try to copy and paste from the internet or copy material out of books, as our Safe-assign Software will soon detect any plagiarism. And that goes for the rest of the class too! Do you all understand me?"

"Yes, Miss Stricto," came the muffled replies.

"Very well. Now you have two weeks to complete the research on your chosen topics. Class dismissed."

Wilbur had the glummest of looks on his face as he went off home, kicking his heels all the way. He soon realised that despite his great enthusiasm for astronomy, he had definitely overstretched himself in choosing to write about different star types. But his teacher, Miss Stricto, would not let him change his topic now.

"Why the miserable look on your face, Wilbur?" his father asked him as the family were seated around the dinner table.

"Have you been causing trouble with Miss Stricto again?" his mother asked.

"He's been too ambitious with his choice of projects and Miss Stricto won't let him change to something simpler," his sister Cathleen giggled.

"Oh shut up Cathleen!" Wilbur burst out.

"You know Mum, everyone at school calls him a fantasist and a dreamboat," continued Cathleen.

"And everyone calls you 'skinny freak,'" retorted her brother.

"Enough you two!" hollered Mr. Barnes.

"Look, Wilbur," began his mother, "what exactly is the problem?"

"Miss Stricto won't let me change my topic assignment."

"And why do you want to change it?"

"Because he discovered that it was too difficult for him," interjected his sister.

"I'll explain to mum, not you, you numbskull."

"That's quite enough fighting, you two," came the authoritative voice of their father.

"Now tell me," said Mrs. Barnes, "why won't Miss Stricto let you change your topic?"

"She said that I have to learn to stick with a topic once I've chosen it," said Wilbur rather ashamedly.

"Well, I agree with Miss Stricto. You can't keep chopping and changing on a whim."

"Now what exactly is your chosen topic Wilbur?" Mr. Barnes asked.

"It's about the different types of stars in the Universe and about how they are born and how they die."

His father gave out a whistle, the kind that usually denotes astonishment. His mother folded her arms, sat back in her chair and rolled her eyes heavenwards. His sister Cathleen simply looked down towards the floor and let out a girlish giggle. Wilbur's reaction was merely to support his head in his hands while his elbows rested on the table. Each member of the family maintained their respective poses for about one minute's duration.

"Well, you certainly over-reached yourself this time, Wilbur," said Mr. Barnes breaking the silence.

"And I don't think he'll ever get himself back again," said Cathleen rather contemptuously.

At that, Wilbur suddenly rose from his chair, banged his fists on the table and said, "I'll show you and I'll show Miss Stricto that I can come up with the information and write an essay on it." With that, Wilbur dashed out of the dining room and upstairs to his room.

"I'll believe it when I see it," his sister called after him.

Questions

1.) Write a short essay of approximately 500 words about Earth's closest neighbour, the moon.

2.) Find out as much as you can about Mars and write an essay of around 500 words about this planet.

3.) What do you know about Jupiter? Get as much information as you can about this giant planet and write an essay about it in approximately 500 words.

Use a variety of sources to obtain your information—books, internet, astronomy magazines, TV programmes and science journals.

An Unexpected Visitor

For about half an hour, Wilbur sat on the side of his bed and thought and thought about how he would tackle this tough assignment. He then crawled into bed and fell asleep while mulling over this project he now felt he had foolishly undertaken.

It would have been about an hour later that he awoke. He did not know why he awoke as he usually slept right through until morning. As he rolled over and tried to get back to sleep again, he heard a strange voice say a rather strange thing.

"O be a fine girl kiss me right now sweetheart." Wilbur sat up in bed with a start! He looked around the room but could see no-one. He tried to get back to sleep again but the same voice uttered the same weird words—"O be a fine girl kiss me right now sweetheart."

"I'll bet that's Cathleen up to her tricks again," said Wilbur as he furiously jumped out of bed. "I'll go through to her room and sort her out!"

"Leave Cathleen to sleep," the mysterious voice commanded him. Wilbur wheeled round to face the other end of his room. Standing next to the window was a sight Wilbur had never seen before. There in front of him was a six foot tall silvery transparent figure glistening and glowing in the moonlight. Wilbur froze to the spot speechless.

"Don't be afraid, Wilbur, I mean you no harm."

At last Wilbur found his voice: "who are you? And what do you want?"

"To help you, Wilbur."

"O be a fine girl kiss me right now sweetheart. Whoever you are, I'm neither a fine nor an 'unfine' girl. In fact, I'm not a girl at all. And I'm not a gay so I don't want to kiss you or be kissed by you."

"Wilbur! You have so much to learn. This is mnemonic for remembering the types of stars in the Universe. Astronomers classify the star types as O B A F G K M R N S."

Wilbur stood agape. His mind began to connect this mysterious being to the tough assignment he had to do.

"My name is Stellarman and I know about your assignment," continued the unexpected visitor.

"But . . . . uh . . . . how do you know?" Wilbur stammered.

"The Universe is full of Miss Strictos, Wilbur."

"Oh! So you know about Miss Stricto?"

"I know about many Miss Strictos, and of course I know about your Miss Stricto."

"Wow!" exclaimed Wilbur.

"And, Wilbur, I know exactly how to deal with the Miss Strictos of this Universe."

"Really?" responded Wilbur, a massive almost semi-malicious smile invading the innocence of his chubby boyish countenance. "But there must be millions or billions of Miss Strictos. How can you deal with them all?"

"I can't. The Celestial Council of Galactic Wanderers draws out a Miss Stricto by lot. You were the lucky winner, Wilbur."

"And how exactly are you going to help me, Stellarman?"

"I'm going to take you on a trip around the galaxy and show you the different types of stars."

"Do you have a spacecraft then?"

"No Wilbur, I don't."

"Then how can we journey around the galaxy without a spacecraft?"

"We will travel through the space-time curvatures of the Universe."

"How shall I breathe and how shall I survive the deadly radiation in space?"

"You will be protected within the curvatures, Wilbur. Have no fear. All you need are your pen and notebook. Are you ready?"

"Yes, but just one more thing."

"What's that?"

"By the time I get back to Earth, my parents and sister will be very old—maybe even dead. You know, I eh mean, relativity and all that."

Stellarman laughed and told Wilbur that while time would advance through one kind of Wormhole, it would regress through another.

"All right, I'm ready, let's go," said Wilbur enthusiastically.

Questions

1.) What is the mnemonic used by astronomers to aid them in remembering the star types?

2.) Wilbur expresses his worry to Stellarman about radiation in space. What do you know about the Van Allen Belts? Find out what you can about them.

O Type Stars

"So what should I do now Stellarman?" Wilbur asked.

"Just come and stand near me." Wilbur walked over to Stellarman and stood beside him. Immediately the silvery light which emanated from Stellarman extended outwards to encapsulate Wilbur. At once, Wilbur and Stellarman rose from the floor and went through the window like light through glass. Soon they were flying through the air.

"Oh! Stellarman. It's all true. You really can fly."

"That's right Wilbur, and you can too."

"Why is it so dark Stellarman? I can't see anything, not even stars?"

"That's because we are now inside a wormhole where space and time are curved? But don't worry Wilbur, you'll soon see something to make your eyes pop."

About half a minute later, Wilbur saw before him a massive blue object. He just stood in awe and gazed at it.

"Stellarman! What is that?!" exclaimed Wilbur.

"That Wilbur is an O type star. This particular one we are looking at is called Zeta Orionis. Now get your pen and notebook ready to take down some information on this type of star."

Wilbur scrambled into his school-bag and shuffled around to find his notebook and pen. He then eagerly awaited information from his mysterious guide.

"The O type stars are the largest of all the star types. Their light is mainly in the ultraviolet and they shine one million times brighter than your sun does."

"How hot are they, Stellarman?"

"They can be between 20 to 100 times the size of your sun and their surface temperatures are between 30,000C to 50,000C. These types of star are very rare as they have a lifetime of only between three to six million years."

"Why so short a lifetime?"

"It is because they burn up their hydrogen fuel so very quickly. Only about one in every three million stars in the main sequence are O type stars."

"Stellarman?" said Wilbur looking at his guide quizzically, "what do you mean by the 'main sequence?'"

"After a star has formed from a collapsing cloud of interstellar gas and dust, it enters what is called the main sequence of the Hertzsprung-Russell Diagram. This is the stage when the star is converting hydrogen into helium by a process of nuclear fusion. This is what gives a star its light and heat."

"I see Stellarman. But now tell me about the Hetzsprung-Russell Diagram."

"This diagram plots the luminosity of stars against their colour. It was named after two scientists who devised it—Ejnar Hertzsprung and Henry Norris Russell. The vertical axis of the graph shows the luminosity of the stars—your sun being classified by the number 1. It is about half way down the vertical axis. The horizontal axis shows the star types, their spectral class and their surface temperatures. The main sequence stars run along a line which extends from the top left hand corner of the graph down to the bottom right hand corner. The main sequence stars are what are termed the dwarf stars."

"Say Stellarman, are there planets around this star we are looking at now?"

"Planets do not form around O type stars because of a process known as photoevaporation."

"Oh! What is that, Stellarman?"

"Planets are stripped of their atmosphere due to high energy protons and electromagnetic radiation. O stars give off so much radiation that it is very difficult for planetary systems to evolve."

"And because these stars are so short lived, there will simply not be enough time for planets to form, I suppose?"

"You are absolutely right Wilbur."

"What is the fate of an O type star, Stellarman?"

"Well, Wilbur, most of them end their lives in a massive supernova explosion."

"And how does that happen?"

"There are two basic types of supernovae. The first kind when the carbon and oxygen in a white dwarf arrive at a critical density. This causes uncontrolled fusion of carbon and oxygen—the result is an explosion. The second type of supernova is connected to massive stars. When they approach the end of their lives and their fuel is exhausted, they leave behind a huge iron core. This core collapses and causes an explosion."

"So when does a star leave the main sequence, Stellarman?"

"It depends upon the initial mass of the star. The more massive the star, the faster it burns up its hydrogen supply and so the faster it leaves the main sequence to become a supergiant or even a hypergiant."

"So stars are composed mostly of hydrogen?"

"Yes, stars begin their lives with about 70% hydrogen and 28% helium with trace amounts of the heavier metals."

"I see."

"This, I think, is enough for the first night, Wilbur."

"What should I do now, Stellarman?"

"Let's go back to your house."

In a few seconds, Wilbur and Stellarman were flying through the time vortex. Soon they were back in Wilbur's room. To Wilbur's surprise, the time was exactly the same as it had been when he had left on the mysterious journey with Stellarman.

"So, what should I do now Stellarman? We still have all the other stars to visit."

"Use the notes that you took tonight when we visited Zeta Orionis to write up the first part of your project assignment."

"I'll do that at school tomorrow. I hope Miss Stricto will be pleased."

"I hope so too, Wilbur. You know though, the Miss Strictos of this Universe are more often than not very hard to please."

"Don't I just know it, Stellarman, don't I just know it?"

"Now then class," began Miss Stricto the following day, "I hope that you have managed to find some information on the topics which you have chosen."

"Yes, Miss Stricto," answered the class in chorus.

"And did you make notes from the various sources which you consulted?"

"Yes, Miss Stricto," came the same choral reply.

"Very well then class, using your notes, start writing now. You have one hour and fifteen minutes."

One hour and fifteen minutes later, Miss Stricto asked the class to stop writing. Everyone put down their pens and awaited to see what she would say next.

"Now then class," began Miss Stricto, "I would like to ask you about the non-internet sources which you consulted when researching your topic. I am not against anyone using the internet, but we must learn to use sources other than online ones. Now then Jonathon, how did you get obtain your information on railway engines?"

"My uncle is a train driver, so I asked him. He said I can interview some railway staff so as to get even more information."

"Splendid Jonathon. Jemimah, what about you?"

"My topic is about the amount and kinds of sweets children eat. So I have devised a questionnaire and handed it to children in this school and the other schools in the area to fill in and hand back to me."

Miss Stricto went round all the 25 children in the class. The 25th one was Wilbur. She gave him a hard piercing look before she finally put the question to him.

"Now then Wilbur. How are you going to remember all the star types in the galaxy?"

Wilbur took a deep breath but hesitated. He was not quite sure how to put it to Miss Stricto.

"Well Wilbur!" shrieked Miss Stricto, "have you lost your tongue?"

At last, Wilbur blurted out, "O be a fine girl kiss me right now sweetheart."

The class was in a complete uproar with all the pupils in hysterical fits of laughter.

"WILLLLLL BURRRR!!" screamed Miss Stricto from the top of her voice, "how dare you, just, just Ohhhh how dare you!"

"But Miss Stricto," whimpered Wilbur.

"Don't you Miss Stricto me, my boy. Go to the headmaster's office this very instance."

Wilbur shuffled out of the class and down the corridor to the headmaster's office where he explained what had happened in class.

"And whatever possessed you to say such a terrible thing to Miss Stricto?" said the headmaster.

"But Mr. Dizplin, it's not what you think," pleaded Wilbur.

"Then what is it Wilbur?"

Mr. Dizplin listened patiently as the boy expounded upon the mnemonic.

"All right Wilbur, let's go and tell all this to Miss Stricto."

The headmaster and pupil walked along the corridor and entered the class. Mr. Dizplin asked Miss Stricto to come out of the class for a private word. A few minutes later, the teacher re-entered the class and asked Wilbur to explain the meaning of his apparently outrageous words. The class was still tittering away at what had happened ten minutes previously and it took Miss Stricto quite some time to settle them all down.

At the end of the day, Wilbur was the butt of every joke. "Who fancies Miss Stricto then?" "Like them old do you?" "When are you and Miss Stricto going to get married then?" were some of the jibes thrown Wilbur's way.

"Anyway," said Wilbur with a disgusted expression stealing across his countenance, "with a face like a fiddle, as skinny as a rake, her piercing eyes staring at you through those thick rimmed triangular glasses that she wears and her hair up in a bun, who would want to kiss the likes of her?—yuck!"

"WILLBURRR," came a voice screaming from a first floor window, "you horrible little boy. I'll see you in the morning. I'll teach you to choose your words more carefully."

"Sorry, Miss Stricto."

"You will be tomorrow morning Wilbur, you will be!"

Can you help Wilbur?

Stellarman took Wilbur to Zeta Orionis and gave him a lot of information about it. However, Miss Stricto is very strict and she will undoubtedly want more than just one example of an O type star.

So, can you help Wilbur? Do your own research and try to find a few examples of O type stars. Give Wilbur information about their sizes, distances from the Earth, their masses, surface temperatures, ages and composition.

B Type Stars

"**Y**ou look rather put out," said Stellarman on his second visit to Wilbur.

"I made a joke about Miss Stricto to the other boys and girls and she overheard me."

"Oh! Don't worry about it Wilbur."

"But she said she's going to see me about it tomorrow."

"Her bark is bigger than her bite. If she mentions it in class, everyone will start laughing and she will only heap more ridicule upon herself."

"I really hope you are right, Stellarman."

"Anyway, forget Miss Stricto and Mr. Dizplin; let's go and visit Regal."

"Who is that?" queried Wilbur with a somewhat puzzled look on his face.

"It's eh a B type star Wilbur," said Stellarman condescendingly.

Stellarman waved his wand and soon he and Wilbur were flying through the time vortex towards Regal.

"It's an amazing star, Stellarman."

"Not quite as big as an O type star—but still very massive.

"How big are they?"

"They range in size from between two to sixteen solar masses."

"Solar masses?"

"This is a way of measuring the sizes of stars by comparing them to your sun. Your astronomers measure a star by saying it is so many times bigger or smaller than the sun."

"So two solar masses means twice the size of the sun and sixteen solar masses means sixteen times the sun's size."

"Absolutely right, Wilbur."

"What kind of surface temperatures do B type stars have?"

"Between 10,000 Kelvin and 30,000 Kelvin. And they are blue in colour."

"And what are they composed of, Stellarman?

"The subclass, B2, show neutral helium in their spectra. They also show a little hydrogen. However, the spectra of the subclass B0 show lines of ionized helium."

"What is 'ionized', Stellarman."

"You know about the table of the elements, don't you Wilbur?"

"Oh yes, our Chemistry teacher, Mr. Toksik, has taught us a lot about it."

"An element becomes ionized when electrons are either added to it or removed from it."

"I see," responded Wilbur. "What other things can you tell me about the stars of this classification?"

"Unlike the sun they do not have a corona."

"What is a corona?"

"A corona is the outer atmosphere of a star—you can see the sun's corona very clearly during a total eclipse. These stars also do not have what is called a convection zone."

"And that is . . . ?"

"First of all let's look at what convection is. It is a means of transporting heat. When a fluid is heated, the hot part rises to the top and cools. The cold part sinks to the bottom. It in turn is heated and rises and so the cycle continues."

"And how does this work in stars, Stellarman?"

"The convection system is one of three ways in which a star carries to its surface the thermal energy which is generated at its core."

"What other ways can this be done?"

"Stars which are of lower mass carry their heat by convective motion, but more massive stars use radiative and conduction methods. In more massive stars, the radiative zones carry the energy generated at the centre of the star by means of photons."

"What are photons?"

"They are bundles (or what physicists call) 'quanta' of light. They are constantly in motion and move at the speed of light."

"And conduction?"

"Metals are very good at conducting heat. Apply a Bunsen burner flame to the bottom of a rod of metal and it soon makes the whole metal rod hot. This is because the atoms are all bumping into each other. The more heat that is applied, the faster the atoms knock against each other and so the rod gets hotter."

"But how can this work in stars?"

"It happens when matter in very massive stars, and also in white dwarfs and neutron stars, becomes very dense. This then becomes what is known as degenerate. Degenerate matter is like metal and is a good conductor of heat. Degenerate matter is created under high pressure conditions where matter is packed tightly together. The most common form of degenerate matter created in the cores of massive stars is metallic hydrogen."

The next day Wilbur walked gingerly into his class. Miss Stricto gave him one of her hard stares through the lenses of her fierce triangular glasses. She said nothing however and Wilbur simply strolled over to his desk.

"Now then class," began Miss Stricto, "would you please continue writing up your essays from your notes?"

After a shuffling of papers and notebooks, Wilbur and the other students embarked upon the task of making their rough notes into legible and meaningful sentences. Miss Stricto slowly walked round the class stopping and stooping to see what the students were doing. Wilbur's desk was situated around the centre of the classroom so when the teacher moved to the back of the class, Wilbur could not see where she was. The boy simply got on with his writing and clean forgot about the old battle ax. Five minutes or so later, he became aware of a presence behind him; he could not see anyone but he was sure of someone standing there. He tried to forget about the presence by applying himself even more assiduously to his writing, but he could not get rid of the awful feeling of being intensely watched. Although it could only have been Miss Stricto, there was something about her that gave Wilbur a dose of the horrors. One minute passed and the boy could bear it no longer; he placed his pen down on the desk and slowly turned round to face the menacing monster behind his chair. He glanced up and found that it was indeed Miss Stricto. But there was something about her that sent a chill down his spine; this middle aged spinster was always considered by her students as being a cold and unfeeling creature, but it seemed to Wilbur that he had caught her just at the instant when these vices had reached a peak of intensity which surpassed all her other moments of malice.

"And how is the Astronomer Royal getting on with his essay?" asked Miss Stricto in highly sarcastic tones. There were stifled giggles from the rest of the class.

"Very well, Miss Stricto," replied Wilbur. "I've written about O type stars and now I'm on to the B ones."

"And eh, from where are you getting all this information Wilbur?"

"Well, eh . . . un . . . er hmm."

"Speak up boy, I asked you a reasonable question."

Miss Wilbur then proceeded to snatch the papers from Wilbur's desk. For about two and a half minutes she perused the text, her hard, cold, malevolent eyes scanning its paragraphs.

"Now then, we do seem to have a budding Astronomer Royal here; but even Astronomers Royal have to reference their works. Now I'll ask you again Sir Wilbur Barnes, what exactly are your sources?"

"Eh hum eh from books and eh from some internet websites."

"Could you show me just one of the books you are currently consulting, Wilbur?"

"Well, I uh haven't brought any books with me."

"Then from where are you getting the information to write these paragraphs?

"I've taken notes. I'm writing them from these notes, see?

Wilbur produced a bundle of notes which he offered to Miss Stricto. She snatched them out of his hands and, with that customary severe look on her taut and rigid countenance, glanced through them.

"These are quite impressive notes, Wilbur. What are the names of the books from where you gleaned this information?"

Wilbur now realised he was in the soup. He thought carefully for a moment and then blurted out—"*Star Types* by Professor Jim Tone."

"I see. So, Professor Jim Tone has been good to you, I see."

"Please Miss," came a rather squeaky voice from the front of the class.

"Yes Cecil Smyth-Tomlinson."

Cecil Smyth-Tomlinson was without doubt the most unpopular boy in the school. In as much as the near inhuman Miss Stricto could ever have a 'pet', Cecil Smyth Tomlinson definitely was the one to be daubed 'the teacher's pet'. The haughty air which he carried around with him and his 'oh so superior' attitude, generally made the flesh of his fellow pupils crawl with putrid disgust. His arrogant face, bedecked with round steel-rimmed glasses, culminated in a long and pointed chin. It was the kind of a face that every pupil felt like giving a good hard punch to.

"Miss Stricto, I have just entered the citation given by Wilbur Barnes in the search engine of my latest smart phone and no results have been found either for the book or the author," came the pompous tones of he with the hyphenated name.

"Now then Wilbur," said Miss Stricto with soft yet threatening tones, "where did you get your information?"

"Em . . . . from . . . . eh . . . Stellarman," replied Wilbur trembling.

"From whom?" asked Miss Stricto straightening up.

"From Stellarman," Wilbur repeated.

"And who exactly is Stellarman?" inquired Miss Stricto, her head placed slightly to the side and the index finger of her right hand on her long, pointed chin.

"He's a kind of galactic wanderer . . . erm . . . he helps children throughout the Universe when they have em em difficult projects to do. He is like glass, ehhh you can see through him."

At this, the class was in a complete uproar. It took all of Miss Stricto's energy to re-instate order.

"Excuse me, Miss Stricto," piped up Cecil Smyth-Tomlinson, "I do declare that Wilbur's imagination has been functioning for excessively long periods on the over-drive mode, so much so that his neurological systems overlap the conscious and the subconscious thus effecting an inability to distinguish between worlds of fantasy and reality."

Wilbur simply stuck out his tongue at Cecil, a response which occasioned the back of his head to come into hard contact with the palm of Miss Stricto's hand.

After school that day, Wilbur walked with positive and determined strides towards the bicycle shed. He did not have a bicycle but he knew that Cecil Smyth-Tomlinson did. Wilbur ensconced himself behind one of the thick pillars which supported the roof of the shed. At last came the moment he was waiting for—Cecil Smyth-Tomlinson entered the enclosure, walked over to his bicycle and started to unchain it—Wilbur emerged from behind the pillar.

"Hello, Honourable Master Cecil Smyth-Tomlinson," said Wilbur in sarcastic tones.

"Whatever do you want with me?" responded Cecil haughtily.

"I want to give you a lesson in astronomy, ponce-boy."

"There are three ways in which I will respond to your unsolicited intrusion: a.) My name is Mr. Cecil Smyth-Tomlinson and not Mr. Ponce-boy. b.) I do not harbour to the slightest degree even a residual interest in the astronomical sciences, and c.) it is still day-light so without the aid of an optical instrument in one form or another, the observation of stars is quite simply an non-accomplishable feat."

Wilbur, completely relaxed and with a contemptuous sneer on his face, started slowly pacing towards his obnoxious class-mate.

"Your name indeed may not be Mr. Ponce-boy and you may indeed not be interested in astronomy, but you are going to see stars in just a few seconds—that is guaranteed."

"Oh really?! And pray tell, what is the instrument by which you will render stellar visibility in the presence of excessive solar light?"

"These," said Wilbur as he bared his fists and sent three punches in rapid succession into Cecil's face. The boy staggered backwards and fell to the ground. On his raising of himself to his feet and on orientating himself in the direction of Wilbur, he revealed to his assailant a black eye, a bleeding nose and massively fat lip.

"You shall render account to the appropriate authorities, Wilbur Barnes, for this unprovoked assault and battery upon my person."

"Aw—go tell mommy about it," laughed Wilbur.

"I shall inform my parents of this outrage without even a modicum of delay."

"Oh, by the way pansy boy—apart from all those glorious stars, did you also chance upon Jupiter and Mars? Ha ha ha!"

"You have not heard the last of this Mr. Barnes."

Wilbur said nothing. He just stuck out his tongue and let fly a loud rasping sound.

"If that is the extent of your vocabulary Barnes, then I can quite easily be forgiven for maintaining in reserve a substantial stock of pity for you."

"And with a face like that, I have a similar stock of the same stuff in reserve for you. In fact, a bit less than before."

"Why? What do you mean?"

"You should thank me for what I've just done?"

"And why-ever should I do that?"

"Because I've made an improvement to your face. You look less girly."

With that, Cecil Smyth-Tomlinson mounted his bicycle and rode off.

Can you help Wilbur?

Find a few more examples of B type stars and help Wilbur by writing up as much information as you can about them.

A Type Stars

"**M**y goodness Wilbur, you do get yourself into some scrapes," said Stellarman on his third visit to Wilbur. "I think there will be serious consequences."

"I don't care now," responded Wilbur huffily. "I hate Cecil Smyth-Tomlinson and I hate Miss Stricto."

"Anyway, I think Cecil Smyth-Tomlinson richly deserved that hiding you gave him."

"Thanks Stellarman. What stars are we going to look at tonight?"

"We are going to visit Gama Cephei, an A type main sequence star."

In a few moments, Wilbur and Stellarman were travelling through the time vortex and soon arrived at the star.

"Oh look Stellarman!" exclaimed Wilbur. It has a planet orbiting around it."

"Yes, most A type stars have planets forming around them. They are young stars, just a few hundred million years old. It is usually massive planets that form around these stars. A types are hydrogen burning stars. Another characteristic of them is that they rotate very quickly. These stars eventually become slower rotating and cooler red giant types. They are between 1.4 to 2 times the mass of the sun. Their surface temperatures range from 7,600K to 10,000K. Do you know what the brightest star in the Earth's skies is, Wilbur?"

"I think it is Sirus, the Dog Star?"

"You are right. It is an A type star and is 25 times brighter than your sun. It is twice the mass of the sun and 1.7 times as big."

"In fact, Sirius is a binary star system."

"Binary star?" queried Wilbur looking rather puzzled.

"A binary star system involves two stars which orbit around each other's centres of gravity. The two stars in the Sirius system are known as Sirius A and Sirius B."

"How long do the two companion stars of Sirius take to revolve around each other."

"Fifty years, Wilbur, fifty years."

"How far is Sirius from the Earth."

"In astronomical terms it is quite close—only 8.5 light years away."

"What other examples of A type stars are there? I know Miss Stricto will want examples.

"Another A type star is Deneb. It is over 1,400 light years away from your planet. Truly it is a massive star—more than 100 times the mass of the sun. An interesting thing about this star is that it has ceased fusing hydrogen in its core."

"So how does it keep burning?"

"No-one is quite sure about that. One theory is that is has started to become cool and to expand into the red supergiant phase. Another theory holds that it has started to fuse helium. It may possibly end its life as a supernova, or it may become a black hole."

"What about Vega? Isn't it an A type star too?"

"Yes indeed it is."

"It is relatively close to your sun—only 25 light years away. It is spinning so rapidly that if it spun any faster it would break up. It has 40 times the brightness of your sun. In about another 400 million years or so it will stop burning its hydrogen and start to burn its supply of helium. It will then become a red giant."

"Can I have just one more example please, Stellarman?"

"Altair is an interesting star. It rotates very rapidly—at around 180 miles per second. That is about half its breakup speed."

"Does our sun rotate as rapidly as that?"

"Oh no, Wilbur. By comparison, your sun is a slow rotator; it rotates at around one and a half miles per second. It completes its rotation in about a month but Altair completes its rotation in a mere ten hours."

"Is it a massive star?"

"No, in fact it is what is called a dwarf star. It is a little bit bigger than your sun but has a surface temperature of around 7,500 degrees Kelvin and is more than ten times brighter than your sun. Altair is what is known as a Cepheid variable star."

"A Cepheid variable?"

"A Cepheid variable is a star whose luminosity can vary in a short period of time. There are many kinds of Cepheid; Altair is what is known as a Delta Scuti variable star."

"How often do Cepheids vary their luminosity?"

"It depends on the type. The Delta Scuti type can vary their luminosity in only a matter of hours—from 0.003 to 0.9. What are termed Type II Cepheids are stars which vary their luminosity in periods ranging from one to fifty days."

"That's amazing, Stellarman."

"Yes. And now I think it is time for you to get home. Enough for tonight."

"Stellarman! I'm so worried about what will happen to me tomorrow."

"Don't worry Wilbur, here is exactly how to handle Miss Stricto et al . . . ."

"Oh yes, Stellarman, that sounds great!" exclaimed Wilbur after ten minutes of listening to his mentor's instructions.

The following day, Wilbur reluctantly trudged his way to class. He was extremely apprehensive about the consequences of his scrape the previous afternoon with Smyth-Tomlinson. In the playground, Wilbur saw Smyth-Tomlinson; he was talking to another boy. In spite of his fear of punishment, Wilbur could not resist having another go at his enemy.

"Well, well, still bearing the scars from last night's supernova explosion," said Wilbur in a mocking tone of voice.

"Oh! Pay no attention to that ruffian," said the boy next to Smyth-Tomlinson.

"Well now, if it isn't Cedric Fortheringay-Jenkins," said Wilbur, his mocking tones metamorphosing into a kind of proto chuckle.

"I have already informed the headmaster of your brutality," said Smyth-Tomlinson.

"Let us depart from hence, Cecil, and cease the wastage of time conversing with such low class and inferior people."

"Goodbye girls!" Wilbur called after them.

Inside the classroom, Wilbur was prepared for the worst. Miss Stricto walked in and eyed the boy down her spectacles.

"Cecil Smyth-Tomlinson, please come to the front of the class," said Miss Stricto.

The boy walked forward towards the teacher. He turned around to reveal to the class a burst nose, two shiners of eyes and a cut lip—the remnants of the previous afternoon's supernova explosion.

"Would you identify the pupil who did this to you?"

"It was that hooligan over there—Wilbur Barnes," he replied pointing at Wilbur.

"Well, Wilbur Barnes," said Miss Strico, her voice piping up, "and what have you got to say for yourself."

"Nothing really. My name is Wilbur Barnes, and I attend the St. Panish Ment School."

"I mean, the assault you perpetrated on this boy yesterday."

"What assault? I had no idea that he was assaulted?"

"Well, look at the condition of his face."

"I see that."

"The how do you explain it?"

"I can't."

"I'll put it to you plainly: did you cause these injuries to Cecil?"

"Does Smyth-Tomlinson have any witnesses he can call?"

"Wilbur Barnes—all you have to do is look at his face."

"He could have had an accident. Maybe he fell of his bike."

"He has clearly been assaulted."

"Even if he has been, that doesn't prove than I was the assailant."

"Did you or did you not punch out Smyth-Tomlinson yesterday?"

"Yes, I did."

"So it is true, you did this to Cecil."

"Not necessarily, Miss Stricto, I could be lying."

"Really?"

"Oh yes; after all, I lied about Jim Tone and you don't believe me about Stellarman, so I may be indulging in false self-accusations."

"But Cecil Smyth-Tomlinson confirms what you have said."

"He could be lying too."

"But . . . ."

"The fact is there are no independent witnesses to back up either of our assertions."

"All right. Sit down, Cecil," said Miss Stricto as the rest of the class were trying to stifle the giggles.

At the end of the day Cecil Smyth-Tomlinson reminded Wilbur that while he may have won a battle, he would not win the war.

Can you help Wilbur?

Find more information about A type stars. Also try to find one or two more examples of them.

VI

F Type Stars

"So what is the next kind of star, Stellarman," Wilbur asked his cosmological guide that evening.

"They are called F type stars Wilbur. Oh! Bye the way, how did things go with Miss Stricto today?"

"I did exactly as you told me to do," replied Wilbur.

"And it worked?"

"Fantastically, Stellarman, fantastically!"

"Let's now get ready to go and visit Procyon A. It is a good example of a type F star."

Through the time vortex went Wilbur and Stellarman and at last they came to Procyon A.

"It's not as big as the others stars we saw," commented Wilbur.

"The F type stars are only about one and a half times the size of your sun," explained stellarman. "They have surface temperatures of between 6000K to 7,500K."

"How distant are they from the Earth?"

"They lie within about 100 or so light years from your planet."

"And what about their luminosities?"

"They are between two to six times the luminosity of your sun. However, they are not as hot as the O, B and A stars so they radiate light at the infrared end of the spectrum. As they are smaller stars, they spend as many as seven to as few as three billion years as hydrogen burners in the main sequence."

"Are all F type stars small?"

"No, there are some F type supergiants. Canopus is an example of such a star. It is nine times more massive than your sun and has a luminosity 15,000 times greater. The spectra of these stars show a preponderance of ionized atoms but few neutral ones. In fact they show ionized calcium in their spectra."

"Do they have planets around them?"

"Oh indeed they do. Extrasolar planet hunters and SETI searchers mainly target those stars. The Spitzer Telescope has detected what are called debris disks around many F type stars. These disks are the leftovers from the gas and dust of the stellar formation process."

"Are these the raw materials for planets?"

"Yes indeed."

"So tell me about all the civilisations in the Universe, Stellarman."

"Let's begin with the basic raw materials for life, life's fundamental building blocks."

"What are these, Stellarman?"

"Bacteria and viruses, Wilbur."

"What?!" exclaimed Wilbur. Simple bacteria are the fundamental building blocks of life?"

"Ah Wilbur, but bacteria are not so simple. They are the very driving force of evolution. Many of the bacteria of which most of the interstellar gas clouds are composed have highly complex DNA."

"What you say is absolutely incredible, Stellarman."

"Two very forward-looking British scientists, Sir Fred Hoyle and Professor Chandra Wickramasinghe, came to this conclusion in 1979. After around 20 years of trying to establish the composition of interstellar space dust, they concluded that it was actually desiccated bacteria."

"What are 'desiccated bacteria'?"

"These are bacteria which are dried out – all the moisture having been removed from them."

"But, wouldn't the bacteria be killed by the heavy exposure to radiation?"

"The bacteria are enclosed in a protective carbonaceous coating. And yes, probably most of the bacteria are indeed killed by radiation, but even if only a small percentage survive, that still leaves an awful lot in terms of cosmological quantities. It should also be remembered that bacteria are very hardy forms of life; they can survive in extremes of hot and cold. Some forms of bacteria actually thrive in nuclear power plants."

"So you mean enough could survive to seed the Universe?"

"Yes, enough to spread life-giving spores throughout the cosmos."

"So has life developed on many planets?"

"Yes, life indeed has. But by 'life' we do not necessarily mean highly evolved intelligent life. Some planets have life which has never developed beyond the bacterial stage—conditions are too harsh. Other planets have managed to give rise to simple plant life; others to more complex plant and insect life. And there are many planets where conditions have been conducive to the evolution of animal life. Throughout the Universe, there are many Earth-like planets where the human species has evolved."

"Are these civilisations more advanced than they are on Earth?"

"They are at many stages of development. Some are still at the Stone Age, some at what would be equivalent to your Medieval era, others are at about your stage of development and a few are much more advanced."

"How does all this fit in with Darwinian evolution?"

"Darwin theorised that life sprung from a 'primordial soup' or 'small warm ponds'. The problem with life arising on a planet is that in terms of time and pre-biotic materials, a planet's resources are insufficient to produce even one single cell, let alone life in all of its complexity. Life therefore requires the resources of the Universe. Genetic material is formed in space, it gives itself expression in multi-celled creatures (plant and animal) on planetary bodies and their satellite moons. As Professors Hoyle and Wickramasinghe said—planets are basically 'assembly stations' for genetic material to express itself in various life forms."

"But what about evolution in increments; I mean Charles Darwin's theory that evolution proceeds over the eons in small imperceptible stages in species?"

"The fossil record does not support that."

"Wasn't Darwin aware of that?"

"Oh yes he was. However, he thought that it would only be a matter of time before the intermediate species were found."

"And were they?"

"In his book *Origin of Species*, Darwin specifically stated that if the intermediate species were not found—'there goes my theory'."

"And . . . . ?"

"Well, 153 years on from the publication of *Origin of Species*, they have never been found."

"I wonder if Darwin would still believe in his theory of evolution if he were alive today."

"It's doubtful that Darwin would be a Darwinist. Darwin's contemporary, Alfred Russel Wallace believed in evolution in quite a different way from which Darwin did. He theorised that evolution occurred in leaps and bounds, not by means of the small incremental stages that Darwin professed. He postulated that species suddenly became extinct and new species suddenly arose."

"What you say, Stellarman, seems to fit better with the fossil record evidence. But why have so many paleontologists been so slow to accept Wallacian Evolution?"

"Old theories that have become so ingrained in the scientific psyche are hard to expunge. I think another reason is that no mechanism has ever been found that would account for the sudden extinction of one species and the sudden emergence of another."

"So what is that mechanism?"

"The theories of Hoyle and Wickramasinghe expostulate a mechanism whereby incoming genetic material in the form of pathogens drives the evolutionary processes."

"But Stellarman! Don't pathogens cause sicknesses that can sometimes prove to be fatal?"

"Yes, that is true. And that is exactly what has happened during many of the Earth's epochs. However, while most living forms are killed off by the incoming pathogens, some are strong enough to actually take advantage of the new DNA and so jump up to the next rung in the evolutionary ladder. Thus Wallace's theory of sudden disappearance and sudden appearance of species is vindicated by the theories of Hoyle and Wickramasinghe."

"So, pathogens from the cosmos providing new genetic material, is the missing mechanistic link from Alfred Russel Wallace's brand of evolutionary theory?"

"Yes. And 'new genetic material' is the key. The shuffling around of genes will simply produce variations within a given species; but if there is to be a jump to the next evolutionary rung, then a fresh injection of genetic material is essential."

"So it seems that Alfred Russel Wallace has been vindicated."

"Yes indeed. Not only on Earth Wilbur. This has been the process of evolution which has been played out on countless planets throughout the cosmos."

"But why isn't it still going on now, Stellarman?"

"Oh it is Wilbur, it is."

"Really?"

"Tell me Wilbur—do you ever catch colds and influenza?"

"Yes, that often happens."

"And how do you get these?"

"Colds and influenza come from viruses. That's what Mr. Deenay our biology teacher told us."

"Did he tell you where they came from?"

"Er . . . no em he didn't."

"Where do you think they come from Wilbur?"

"They are eh just around in the air, I suppose."

"And how do you catch illnesses like colds, flus, whooping cough and measles?"

"They are contagious. We catch them from other people who are infected."

"It will surprise you Wilbur when I tell you that this is a common fallacy. Pathogens which cause these common ailments come from space. They are brought by comets. When the patterns of epidemics are analysed carefully, there is almost no evidence of person to person transmission. Shepherds and crofters living in remote areas who have no contact with people for weeks on end succumb to these flu epidemics. And people who live in close contact with infected people completely escape the ravages of these sicknesses."

"That's an astonishing insight, Stellarman."

"The insight is to be credited to Hoyle and Wickramasinghe. Read their book *Diseases from Space*; it will be a real eye-opener for you Wilbur."

"Thanks Stellarman. I'll try to get hold of it."

"It is amazing how the two authors, astronomers by training and profession, put the whole science of epidemiology into a completely new context—a cosmological context."

"Is there any sort of direct evidence of space-borne diseases?"

"Spectroscopic analyses of interstellar dust dovetail with those for desiccated bacteria. In fact, E. Coli seems to be prevalent in the cores of comets and in objects as distant as the Trapezium Nebula which is a part of the Orion Nebula."

"You have given me a lot of food for thought, Stellarman. I've got plenty to write about in class tomorrow."

"So life comes from outer-space, does it Wilbur?" said Wilbur's father the following evening at the dinner table."

"Um eh yes," said Wilbur somewhat taken aback by what his father had just said. "How do you know this, Dad? I mean, you're not interested in science."

"Stellarman told us, Wilbur."

At this revelation, Wilbur almost fell off his chair. He blushed a deep crimson-red as he almost choked on the morsel of meat he had just half swallowed.

"But how do you know Stellarman?"

"From you Wilbur," said his sister Cathleen.

"Cathleen has been hearing you talk in your sleep these past few nights Wilbur," the boy's mother explained.

"We listened outside your door to your imaginary conversations with your equally imaginary friend, Stellarman," said Cathleen.

"But . . . . but . . ." spluttered Wilbur, "how could you have heard me when I had travelled through the time and space vortex and was many light years away?"

"You hadn't travelled anywhere, Wilbur," said Mrs. Barnes.

"Except in your dreams," added his sister with a sneer.

"But I wasn't in my room," pleaded Wilbur.

"Well your mother, sister and I looked in and saw you snuggly tucked up in bed," said Mr. Barnes.

"And blabbering away to Mr. Stellarman," said Cathleen.

Wilbur said nothing more. He hurriedly finished his evening meal and darted towards the door.

"Where are you going, Wilbur?" asked his father.

"I'm going to the library," responded Wilbur.

"Are you going to be meeting Stellarman there?" asked his sister sarcastically.

Wilbur, with his essay and notes under his arm, turned on his heels and headed to the library. On his way to the library, Wilbur felt a cloud of mixed emotions descend upon him. He was angry, yet deeply depressed. Was Stellarman a dream? What kind of information had his mind's subconscious been feeding him in the personification of 'Stellarman'?

Wilbur must have spent three hours in the library. He was a good researcher and used both astronomy books and the internet to find out what he wanted. However, there was one particular book that he desperately wanted to get hold of.

"Excuse me Miss," said Wilbur to the librarian.

"Yes, young man. How can I help you?"

"I need a book entitled *Diseases from Space* by Sir Fred Hoyle and Chandra Wickramasinghe.

The librarian got on to her computer and started looking. After a few minutes she told the lad that this book was in the stacks—in the basement of the library.

"Here's a torch Wilbur. Go down and look for it yourself. It's been out of print for many years. I'll open up for you. I'll give you fifteen minutes to find it."

The stacks was a dark and creepy place. However, Wilbur being Wilbur would not be deterred. He soon found what he had been looking for and rushed up to the main part of the library. For a whole hour and a half more he skimmed and scanned the book and made notes of what he had found to be of interest in it. After four and a half hours in the library Wilbur started on his way home.

This time his mood had completely changed. Everything that Wilbur had researched on O, B, A, and F stars corresponded perfectly to what Stellarman had told him. And there was nothing in *Diseases from Space* that contradicted anything that his mysterious friend had said concerning the theories of its two authors. Figment of the imagination or no figment of the imagination, everything Stellarman had taught him seemed to be bona fide stuff.

"I'm for real alright," came a voice from behind Wilbur.

"Stellarman!" exclaimed Wilbur.

"Not too loudly Wilbur. You can see me but others can't."

"I'm not sure if all this is a dream or reality."

"I'll explain all tomorrow, Wilbur."

"Aren't we going to be looking at G type stars tonight?"

"Give it a break for tonight Wilbur. I want you to digest everything we have talked about so far."

The next morning, Wilbur noticed that quite a few of the pupils in the school playground were looking in his direction and sniggering.

"What's so funny?" he asked a huddled and giggling group.

"It's about your friend, Stellarman."

"Who told you about Stellarman?" Wilbur demanded.

"Your two best friends," said one of the pupils.

"Cecil Smyth-Tomlinson and Cedric Fortheringay-Jenkins," said another.

Wilbur scoured the playground until at last he found who he was looking for.

"You pair of gossiping faggots," said Wilbur through clenched teeth.

"Pray what is the meaning of this outburst, Barnes?" asked Smyth-Tomlinson.

"Who told you about Stellarman?"

"Your sister Cathleen of course," came the answer from Fortheringay-Jenkins.

"I'll get you two for that. I'll teach you to have the whole school laughing at me."

"Your threats have been well noted Barnes," said Smyth-Tomlinson.

"And shall be dealt with in the appropriate manner," added Fortheringay-Jenkins.

"Cathleen!" screamed Wilbur at his sister, when he had located her. "Why did you tell those two pansies about Stellarman?"

"But they promised to keep it a secret," pleaded Cathleen.

"Oh Cathleen, Cathleen," said Wilbur shaking his head. "You really are pathetic."

At the end of the day, Cecil Smyth-Tomlinson and Cedric Fortheringay-Jenkins made their way to the bicycle shed.

"I dare say," began Fortheringay-Jenkins, "that Wilbur Barnes will not attack us if we proceed as two to collect our bicycles."

"I should well imagine that the two of us should be a deterrence factor, right?"

"Wrong!" came a voice from behind them.

"Keep away from us, you hooligan!" hollered Smyth-Tomlinson.

"I will, after I've shown you both some more stars." And with that, Wilbur punched and kicked them until their faces were well and truly messed up.

"You shall not get away with it this time, you brute", warned Fortheringay-Jenkins.

"Oh! Where are your witnesses?" laughed Wilbur.

"That CCTV camera up there which the headmaster had installed yesterday," said Fortheringay-Jenkins pointing upwards to the top of a wall. With that, Cecil and Cedric dusted themselves down and rode off on their bikes.

Poor Wilbur! Now he knew he was in real trouble. It was all on camera and there was no way he could wiggle out of it with clever legalistic arguments.

Can you help Wilbur?

Find some more examples of F type stars.

What do you know about the SETI project?

What do you know about the famous "Wow signal."

Do you think there are intelligent beings living on planets in other solar systems? If so, what do you think they are like?

Can you write about 1,000 words describing an imaginary encounter with ET?

VII

G TYPE STARS

"**M**y goodness, Wilbur. You do have a pugilistic nature!" said Stellarman when he visited Wilbur that evening. "You should have taken up boxing rather than astronomy!"

"I'm really in for it now, Stellarman. It was all caught on camera."

"Don't worry about it, Wilbur. I'll take care of that."

"How will you do that, Stellarman?"

"Trust me, Wilbur. Just trust me."

"OK," said Wilbur shrugging his shoulders but not fully believing that his friend could really get him off the hook.

"Tonight we are going to take a look at G type stars."

"Before we do that, Stellarman, weren't you going to explain to me how my family saw me sleeping in my bed, apparently talking in my sleep, yet I felt fully awake and millions of light years away."

"The world of Quantum Physics is a strange place, Wilbur. A particle can in fact be observed in two places at the same time. In the bizarre world of Quantum Physics, what we call 'common sense' completely breaks down. There is definitely an overlap between human consciousness and reality at subatomic level."

"Can you give me an example of that, please?"

"Photons of light passed through two slits will either go to the right or left. We can observe which direction they took from a photographic plate placed behind the slits. But a photon will not make that decision until it is actually observed."

"So can the observer determine which direction it will take?"

"No—but the act of observation influences the photon to go one way or the other."

"I'm fascinated, Stellarman, but how does all this fit into my predicament?"

"We Stellarmen can actually do at the macroscopic level what most advanced civilisations can only do at the subatomic level."

"So this is why I can be sound asleep in bed, yet trillions of miles away from the Earth at the same time?"

"Exactly!"

"But am I just dreaming all this or is it real?"

"What is the difference between dreams and reality? In the world of Quantum Mechanics remember, common sense breaks down and the artificial distinction between 'reality' and 'dreams', the 'conscious' and the 'subconscious' all break down."

"I understand better now, Stellarman."

"Let's go to a G type star."

"What is the name of this star?" asked Wilbur as he and his friend floated in space looking at the huge ball of fire before them.

"Different peoples on different planets call it by a variety of names—you guys just call it 'the sun'."

"So the sun is a G type star, is it?"

"Yes it is."

"What is the sun's surface temperature?"

"G type stars have surface temperatures ranging from between 5,330 Kelvin and 6,000 Kelvin."

"Does it convert hydrogen into helium?"

"Yes. It converts hydrogen into helium at its core by a process of nuclear fusion. Every second it fuses 600 million tons of hydrogen to helium. And also every second, it converts four million tons of matter into energy."

"Is our sun what is called a 'yellow dwarf'."

"More strictly speaking, it is a 'white dwarf'. It is only the Earth's atmosphere that causes the sun to appear to be yellow."

"So how exactly does the sun convert hydrogen into helium?"

"About 25% of the radius of the sun is made up of what we call the core. The temperature at the core is very high—more than 15 million degrees Kelvin. Gravity at the core is so strong that it pulls the mass of the sun towards it. The pressure caused by this gravitational pull causes hydrogen atoms to fuse together. Two protons fuse to create what is called a deuterium atom?"

"What is a deuterium atom?"

"It is an isotope of hydrogen. Most hydrogen does not have a neutron in its nucleus but deuterium does in fact have a neutron as well as a proton."

"So what happens next?"

"A proton and a deuterium atom combine to form what is called helium-3."

"Which is . . . ?"

"An atom with two protons and one neutron. The two helium-3 atoms combine to from helium-4. It has two protons and two neutrons. Eighty five percent of the sun's energy is generated by this process."

"What about the other fifteen percent?"

"Heavy elements are formed. A helium-3 and a helium-4 atom fuse together to create beryllium-7. This atom has four protons and three neutrons. It then captures an electron which changes it to lithium-7 which has three protons and four neutrons. The lithium-7 then captures a proton to form two helium-4 atoms."

"What is the 'solar wind', Stellarman?"

"This comes from the highly energized particles called neutrinos and protons which the sun emits. This is what causes the changes in the Earth's weather patterns."

"What about man-made carbon emissions being the cause of climate change?"

"It is all nonsense and politically motivated. The anthropogenic effect is negligible to nil. It is the sun which drives terrestrial weather patterns."

"How long does a G type star last for?"

"It burns hydrogen for around ten billion years. The star then expands to become what is called a red giant."

"When will the sun do this?"

"Your sun is about half way through its life. It will not develop into the red giant stage for another 5 billion years."

The following day, Wilbur had to face the music with regard to Smyth-Tomlinson and Fortheringay-Jenkins.

"Wilbur Barnes!" squawked Miss Stricto.

"Yes Miss Stricto," responded Wilbur in a somewhat bleating voice.

"The headmaster, Mr. Dizplin would like to see you now. Cecil Smyth-Tomlinson and Cedric Fortheringay-Jenkins, you are both also required to be in the headmaster's office along with Wilbur Barnes."

The three pupils walked out of the classroom and along the corridor to Mr. Dizplin's office. Smyth-Tomlinson and Fortheringay-Jenkins looked at Wilbur with that smarmy look which seemed to say 'you've had it now Barnes, we've got you this time.'

"Come in," Mr. Dizplin called out when Smyth-Tomlinson had knocked on the headmaster's door.

"You wanted to see us, Mr. Dizplin," said Fortheringay-Jenkins in a voice of semi-triumphalism.

"Yes indeed. Now you Cecil and you Cedric were given a good beating yesterday afternoon."

"Indeed we were and it was that hooligan . . . ." responded Smyth-Tomlinson.

"Ah now, before you make any accusations as to who perpetrated this assault upon you," said Mr. Dizplin cutting off Smyth-Tomlinson, "I would like to know what evidence you could present to back up any such accusation."

"Please sir, it was all caught on the CCTV camera which you yourself installed."

"Mr. Dizplin sir, if you could play back the events of yesterday afternoon, you will see that the person who brutalised us was none other than . . ."

"Ah ah ah ah ah," interrupted Mr. Dizplin, raising his headmasterly forefinger, "no accusations please."

"But have you seen the playback, sir?" inquired Fortheringay-Jenkins.

"Yes, I have."

"So you know the identity of the brute who assaulted us."

"I *saw* who assaulted you; as to her identity—well, eh, that is another matter."

"Excuse me sir," said Smyth-Tomlinson looking somewhat puzzled. "Her?!"

"But it was Wilbur Barnes who assaulted us," said Fortheringay-Jenkins."

"Be careful whom you are accusing," cautioned Mr. Dizplin.

"But sir, if you replay the film, it will clearly show the culprit."

"Well, I already have done. Anyway, let's see it again."

The headmaster activated his desktop computer and started the playback. It was as much to the utter shock and astonishment of Wilbur Barnes as it was to Smyth-Tomlinson and Fortheringay-Jenkins when clearly shown on the monitor was a girl of around ten years of age kicking and punching at Smyth-Tomlinson and Fortheringay-Jenkins. Wilbur then remembered what Stellarman had told him the previous evening which was that he would take care of the CCTV camera.

"I don't understand sir," pleaded Smyth-Tomlinson.

"Neither do I," responded the headmaster. "Can you shed any light on this matter, Wilbur?"

"Only star-light, sir. I mean the stars Cecil and Cedric saw when they were beaten up by a little girl."

The headmaster let out a wry smile while Smyth-Tomlinson and Fortheringay-Jenkins haughtily turned their heads away.

"Do any of you three boys know the identity of the girl?" asked Mr. Dizplin.

All three boys merely shook their heads.

"Go back to your class boys."

On the way back to class, Wilbur looked at his two enemies with a sneer and said, "If you two cause me any more trouble I'm going to set my little sister on you. Maybe my great-grandma as well!"

Can you help Wilbur?

So then, what is the most well-known G star of all?! How far is it from the Earth?

What are sun spots?

What are solar prominences?

How do eclipses occur?

VIII

K Type Stars

"**M**y goodness, Stellarman!" exclaimed Wilbur, "how did you do it? I was ever so worried when I was called to the headmaster's office."

"Oh Wilbur, we Stellarman are very inventive."

"I can see that. Thanks a lot Stellarman, you certainly got me off the hook."

"So what kind of star are we going to look at tonight?"

"Let's go through the time vortex and visit Sigma Draconis which is a typical K type star."

"So what can you tell me about this star?" asked Wilbur as they floated in space in front of the burning ball of fire.

"It is a main sequence star and is often called an orange dwarf. Their masses are from 0.6 to 0.9 times that of your sun."

"What about their surface temperatures?"

"Their surface temperatures range from between 3,900 Kelvin to 5,200 Kelvin."

"What about their life span?"

"In fact they live a bit longer than G type stars like your sun. While solar type stars have a life of 10 billion years, these K stars range from 15 to as many as 30 billion years."

"And do they have planetary systems and, if so, life on any of the planets orbiting them?"

"Yes. Because they are stable and long-lasting, life is able to take root on planets located within the habitable zones of these stars. The most advanced civilisations in the Universe are found on planets around such stars, again because of the stability and longevity of stars in this category."

"Are there many K type stars in the galaxy?"

"Oh yes. In fact there are between three and four times as many of these types of stars than there are of G types."

"This means a lot of life in the Universe?"

"Yes. It means the Universe is teeming with life—and with human life as well as with life in its lower forms."

"What about the composition of these stars?"

"Spectroscopic analyses of these stars indicate the presence of calcium, neutral iron, magnesium and titanium. They also indicate the presence of cyanogens (CN) and titanium dioxide (TiO). At their cores, they emit energy by the convective process whereas in their outer layers the radiative process comes into play."

When Stellarman and Wilbur returned home, Wilbur seemed rather disturbed about something.

"Tell me Wilbur," said Stellarman, seeing the look on his friend's face. "You seem to be hot and bothered about something."

"You know Stellarman, you've been so kind to me and so helpful, but Miss Stricto insists on a list of references for our sources of information. I've told her all about you, but Miss Stricto gets angry and the class just laugh at me. What can I do?"

"Trust me, Wilbur. I'm working on a plan to help you. So please just be patient."

"I will be, Stellarman."

"And another thing Wilbur."

"Yes, Stellarman."

"Try not to get into any more fights."

"I'll try not to, but it's just that Smyth-Tomlinson and Fortheringay-Jenkins keep picking on me."

"Keep a distance from them Wilbur, keep a good distance from them."

"Sure."

"Now let me give you some advice about the referencing . . . ."

"Now then class," began Miss Stricto the following morning, "I have read through the school's intranet system what you all have written for your assignment projects so far. Today I want to ask you about your sources."

The pupils told Miss Stricto about the books, websites, magazines, journals, DVDs and other source materials they had consulted for their projects. Last of all, she came to Wilbur.

"Well now Wilbur, what about *your* sources?"

Wilbur remained silent for a few seconds. When he saw that Miss Strico was becoming impatient, he mustered the courage to speak up.

"Miss Stricto, for the moment my sources must remain confidential. On the completion of my assignment, I shall provide a full bibliography of all source material consulted."

"Wilbur, when I ask you to provide me with information, you do so without further argument."

"But the latest copyright laws do not require an author to reveal his sources until such times as his material is ready for publication."

"Wilbur Barnes, you do have pretensions above your ability. This is merely a class assignment, not a scholarly work to be presented for publication."

"But I intend it for publication, Miss Stricto."

"And do you seriously think that any publisher is going to accept your work?"

"Perhaps not Miss Stricto, but my intention for this work is publication and so I am covered by the copyright and publication legislation."

"You are a proper little smarty-pants," blurted out Miss Strico forgetting herself.

"I am still under the protection of the copyright laws, Miss Stricto, my pants being smart or otherwise."

The class started tittering as Miss Stricto haughtily turned towards the blackboard. Wilbur sat there at his desk feeling rather pleased with himself.

"I don't think that Miss Stricto is going to accept my excuse for too long," said Wilbur to Stellarman that evening.

"You mean regarding the copyright laws?" queried Stellarman.

"Yes. I'm sure she'll get the headmaster to pressure me on it."

"I think so too. It seems from what you say that you really humiliated that proper madam today."

"Exactly! That is why I'm sure she'll be devising ways to get her own back on me."

"Yes, I wouldn't discount that possibility Wilbur."

"What am I going to do?!" exclaimed Wilbur throwing up his hands in exasperation.

Stellarman thought hard for a few minutes. Wilbur did not interrupt his thoughts. He could see that his galactic friend was working out the next move in the chess game with Miss Stricto.

"Now then!" said Stellarman all of a sudden.

Wilbur who had been sitting on the side of his bed, chin in hands while in a somewhat gloomy reverie, at once perked up and gave his full attention to Stellarman.

"Listen carefully, Wilbur," said Stellarman. "Here is what we are going to do." Stellarman then explained in detail the plan which he had thought up.

"That's a brilliant idea!" exclaimed Wilbur at the top of his voice. "Absolutely brilliant."

"Now let's take a look at the next type of star."

Can you help Wilbur?

Find some more examples of K type stars. Find examples of both long and short lived ones.

IX

M Type Stars

"So what can you tell me about M type stars, Stellarman."

"The majority of main sequence stars are of this classification. In fact around 76% of them. Because of their rather low luminosities, it is impossible to see them with the naked eye. Now let's travel through the space-time vortex to Proxima Centauri."

When Wilbur and Stellarman arrived at Proxima Centauri, Wilbur commented on how small it was in comparison to the other stars that they had visited.

"Most M type stars are red dwarfs," Stellarman explained to his friend. "This star is the nearest to your sun—just over 4 light years away. Its mass is only about an eighth of the sun's but it has 40 times the density. Proxima Centauri is known as a 'flare star.'"

"What does that mean?"

"It means that because of magnetic activity, the star's brightness varies a lot."

"And what causes this magnetic field, Stellarman?"

"This is caused by convection. The star therefore flares a lot and so gives out a lot of X-ray emission. And there is something fascinating I must tell you about this star Wilbur."

"Oh, what is that, Stellarman?"

"A combination of a mixing of the fuel at the star's core and a low energy production, will ensure that this star will remain in the main-sequence area for another four trillion years."

"Four trillion years!" exclaimed Wilbur.

"Yes", replied Stellarman, "and here is something to astound you even more—that is 300 times the present age of the entire Universe."

"That's quite astonishing, Stellarman. You say that although most M type stars are red dwarfs, not all of them are."

"That's correct, Wilbur. Take Alpha Herculis. It is classified as a 'giant.' If it were placed where your sun is now, its radius would extend beyond the orbit of the planet Mars."

"Will it, like Proxima, last another four trillion years?"

"Not this star. In fact, it is now near the end of its life."

"It's ever so big."

"But I'm going to take you to Betelgeuse—it's even bigger still."

When Wilbur and Stellarman arrived at Betelgeuse, Wilbur was in awe at the size of this sun.

"Its classification is that of a 'super-giant,' Wilbur."

"If it were where our sun is, it would engulf much of the solar system, I suppose."

"You are right. Its radius would extend probably even beyond the orbital plane of the giant planet Jupiter."

"Is this star also near the end of its life?"

"Very near its end. It is most likely to explode as a supernova in about one million years time."

"Now let's visit VY Canis Majoris."

"Oh wow, Stellarman. This star is even larger than Betelgeuse."

"Beltegeuse is a super-giant, but this star has the designation 'hyper-giant.'"

"And how far would its radius extend were in placed in our solar system?"

"Most likely beyond the orbit of Saturn. In fact, it is the largest known star in terms of its radius."

"And what is its life expectancy?"

"Even less than that of Betelgeuse. It is expected to explode as a hypernova in as little as 100,000 years. In fact, it may even create a very big black hole."

"I take it that a hypernova is a stellar explosion which is even greater than that of a supernova."

"Absolutely right, Wilbur. It is thought that the long duration gamma ray bursts are due to hypernova explosions."

"I'm a little confused, Stellarman," said Wilbur when they had returned home.

"What about?" asked Stellarman.

"We have seen three different sizes of M type stars. What is their common characteristic?"

"They are classified as such by their spectral lines which indicate absorption bands of titanium oxide and vanadium oxide."

"Now then Wilbur?" began Miss Stricto the following day, "are you going to tell us about your sources of information?"

"No, Miss Stricto. I am covered by the copyright laws."

"Miss Stricto," piped up Cecil Smyth-Tomlinson.

"Yes, Cecil?" responded Miss Stricto.

"I have performed some research on the internet regarding the copyright laws and they do not apply to school essays or to minors under the age of 18."

"Thank you, Cecil," said Miss Stricto smiling on her pet. Turning to Wilbur with a scowl on her fact, she demanded of him to disclose the whereabouts of his information.

"It is Stellarman," said Wilbur curtly.

"The same Stellarman whom you told us about before, Wilbur."

"Yes," responded Wilbur tersely through gritted teeth.

"Perhaps we could see your famous Stellarman some time Wilbur," said Miss Stricto sarcastically.

"You will, Miss Stricto, I promise you—you will."

At the end of the school day, Wilbur went straight to the bicycle shed. He knew that he had a little bit of business with his old foe, Smyth-Tomlinson. However, Smyth-Tomlinson was not there—and neither was his bike.

"Peculiar," thought Wilbur to himself. After a few moments of puzzlement, it dawned on Wilbur that Smyth-Tomlinson had ran quickly for his bike and peddled off as fast as he could. Wilbur darted off as fast as his legs could carry him. Instead of leaving the school premises through the main gate, Wilbur dashed for the wall at the back of the school. Heaving an old oil drum from near the janitor's office, he clambered on to it and heaved himself up to the top of the wall. He then proceeded along the length of the wall until he got to a tree. He jumped onto one of its branches and, in monkey style, walked his hands along its length until he got to the trunk. With great agility he slithered down the tree-trunk and waited behind the tree.

Wilbur's timing was spot on. A minute later Smyth-Tomlinosn came peddling up the street on his bicycle. His nose in the air and smug look on his face, were the symptoms of satisfaction his feeling of having outsmarted his rival engendered within him.

This subjective feeling of well-being however was soon shattered when Wilbur, after moving from behind the tree, jumped on top of his enemy and knocked him clean off of his bicycle.

"You hooligan, you lout!" screamed Smyth-Tomlinson when he picked himself up and came to his senses.

"I'm going to teach you once and for all that interfering in my assignment is just not on", said Wilbur with perfect calmness in his demeanour. "Now do you know the differences between novas, supernovas and hypernovas?"

"I have made it plain to you on other occasions, Wilbur Barnes, that I am not the least bit interested in astronomy."

"Oh yes you are," responded Wilbur somewhat wryly.

"What arrogance!" blurted out Smyth-Tomlinson. "Do you think you know better than I do what I am and what I am not interested in?"

"But you have displayed your interest in astronomy a number of times in the classroom."

"Whatever do you mean?"

"The times when you told Miss Stricto that my sources were bogus can be validly interpreted as a display of interest in the subject. Otherwise, why would you care about the authenticity of my sources?"

Smyth-Tomlinson was stumped at this unexpected morsel of wisdom proceeding from the one whom he always considered as being 'a moron.'

"Now then," continued Wilbur, "back to business. Tell me about the three types of nova I mentioned a moment ago."

"I would think that the differences are in intensity of explosion," said Smyth-Tomlinson.

"Yes," responded Wilbur tersely. "Now do you believe that pedagogical points in a lesson should be given practical demonstration for the purposes of emphasis and cognitive retention?"

"I cannot dispute the validity of these methodoligical techniques."

"Oh good, gooooood," said Wilbur quite calmly and collectedly. "Now that is a nova," he explained as he punched Smyth-Tomlinson on the left eye. "And that is a supernova explosion," he said punching his foe even harder on the right eye. "And *that!*" he yelled as his fist lammed onto Smyth-Tomlinson's nose, "is undoubtedly a hypernova explosion."

"I'm going to get my father to come to the school. You will be dealt with severely," bawled Smyth-Tomlinson. "And you've broken my bicycle, you vandal."

"You have no witnesses," retorted Wilbur.

"Oh yes he has," came the voice of Cedric Fortheringay-Jenkins. Wilbur's other foe rode along the street on his bicycle; with one hand on a handlebar and the other in the air, he flashed a mobile phone in front of Wilbur and informed him that the whole incident had been recorded on the phone's video facility. "I saw the fracas from a distance and hid myself behind a tree and recorded everything."

Smyth-Tomlinson's pain was eased somewhat as a vestige of the smugness returned to his bruised and battered countenance. Wilbur's elation gave way to extreme anxiety as he knew that the camera could not lie.

Can you help Wilbur?

Find some more examples of M type stars. Find out more information about nova types of stellar explosion. What do you know about the Crab Nebula?

R, N AND S TYPE STARS

"**Y**ou seem to be a boy who likes a scrap, Wilbur," said Stellarman when he came to visit Wilbur that evening.

"Stellarman! Believe me, I'm not, but those two interfering busybodies needed to be taught a lesson. Oh Stellarman, please help me."

"All right, Wilbur, all right. But only because you are in the right!"

"Thanks, Stellarman. You're a real pal."

"And tonight we are going to learn about carbon stars."

"Are these the R type stars?"

"Well, yes, but there have been so many sub-types discovered that the final three older forms of classification have been eliminated."

"So what is the first kind of star we will look at?"

Wilbur and Stellarman went through the vortex to a star which Stellarman named as Monocerotis.

"Monocerotis is what is now called an L type star."

"It is very big," commented Wilbur.

"It is a supergiant. It was discovered as recently as 2002. When astronomers observed it, they thought at first that it was experiencing a nova type explosion, but on closer examination it did not appear to bear the hallmarks of a typical nova eruption. The consensus opinion among astronomers is that this star is in its final death throes. It was discovered in January and had brightened substantially by February. It then started to decrease in luminosity. It started to brighten again in

March, but by April it had increased its brightness to a million times that of solar luminosity."

"Oh wow! It must have been one of the brightest stars in the galaxy."

"Indeed it was, Wilbur. However, it then returned to more or less its original luminosity. It became cool and red thus becoming the first observed L type supergiant."

"What can we say about L type stars generally, Stellarman?"

"They are generally dwarf type stars. They are deep red and show alkali metals and metal hydrides in their spectra."

"What other kind of stars are there?"

"There are the Class T Methane types. They are cool brown dwarfs and, as their name suggests, they have an abundance of methane in their spectra. Then we have what are termed Y stars. These are brown dwarfs too but cooler than the T dwarfs."

"What kind of temperatures do brown dwarfs usually have?"

"Around 500 to 600 Kelvin."

"That's cool compared to the temperatures on the O, B and M type stars."

"Yes, indeed. The stars that were once classified as R and N types, are now designated 'carbon stars.'"

"And I take it that this is because of large quantities of carbon in their atmospheres."

"Yes, that is correct. These stars are mainly red giants or supergiants which are near the end of their lives."

"What about S stars?"

"These stars show zirconium monoxide in their specra. Their carbon and oxygen are mostly in the form of molecules of carbon monoxide. Like other carbon stars, these S types are either giants or supergiants."

As Wilbur walked into the precincts of his school the following morning, he heard the familiar 'beep beep' of his mobile phone. On extricating it from his pocket, he looked to see who could be texting him at this time of the day. It turned out that it was a video that had been sent to him. After watching it, he burst into a fit of giggles. He then looked around the playground for his two 'friends.' On finding them, he queried of them as to whether they were sure they wanted to involve parental and school authority in the matter of their most recent duffing up.

"Why should we not, Barnes? The incriminating evidence is all here on videophone," said Fortheringay-Jenkins.

"Really now?" responded Wilbur, "but I have some incriminating stuff on *my* mobile phone. Take a gawk at this."

To their shock and consternation, Smyth-Tomlinson and Fortheringay-Jenkins saw themselves at a ballet school learning how to pirouette and balance on their toes.

"Now I didn't know that you two fairies did ballet," sneered Wilbur.

"We do not; this video is pure fakery," protested Smyth-Tomlinson.

"And so is your video then. Oh! And by the way, what will everyone say about your green tights, Cedric? And your pink ballet pumps, Cecil?"

"I tell you, it is a fraud," said Fortheringay-Jenkins.

"We have evidence of your assault upon me yesterday afternoon," said Smyth-Tomlinson.

At this, Fortheringay-Jenkins whipped out his mobile phone from his pocket, searched for the appropriate video and held it up to Wilbur.

"Now just take a look at that, Wilbur Barnes," uttered Fortheringay-Jenkins in triumphant tones. Isn't it incriminating?"

"Indeed it is, indeed it is," replied Wilbur. "Incriminating you two."

"Huh! Whatever do you mean?" asked Smyth-Tomlinson

"That video should put the worries into you," said Fortheringay-Jenkins.

"Nope!" replied Wilbur quite calmly, "but it should put the worries into you two."

"You are desperate Barnes," said Fortheringay-Jenkins as he pulled the phone away from Wilbur's face.

"Oh no!" said Wilbur completely relaxed. "Why don't you two fairies take another look at that video?"

The faces of Wilbur's two foes went crimson-red. On looking at the video, they once again saw themselves at the ballet class and dancing around in their pink-coloured tights.

"But how?!" said Smyth-Tomlinson and Fortheringay-Jenkins in unison.

"Hee heee heee heeeee—dunno," tittered Wilbur.

Smyth-Tomlinson then took out his mobile phone and started dialing. He put it to his ear and after a few moments said, "eh, hello Dadsie. I don't think it will be necessary for you to come to school after all. Cecil and I have sorted things out with Wilbur Barnes."

Wilbur walked off chuckling away to himself. He had gained yet another victory over his two deadly foes. However, a few minutes later, Wilbur's phone rang.

"Hello. Who is this?" asked Wilbur. Wilbur was somewhat puzzled as no number had appeared on the phone.

"It's me—your friend," came the voice.

"Stellarman!" said Wilbur in an exclaimed whisper.

"You didn't hear the whole conversation between Cecil and his father, did you?"

"No, I walked away in a fit of giggles," said Wilbur.

"Well, I want you to listen to it. I made a recording of it."

"All right."

Father: So you have become friends with Wilbur Barnes?

Cecil: Not exactly Papa.

Father: Then what do you mean when you say that you have 'sorted things out' with him?

Cecil: I challenged him to a fight in the playground this morning.

Father: What?! You challenged him to fight?!

Cecil: Yes.

Father: And what was the outcome?

Cecil: I gave him the hiding of his life. He was begging for mercy. 'Enough, enough,' he cried. 'I know when I'm licked.'

Father: Oh you brave boy Cecil. Well done.

Cecil: He promised me he would never bother me again. 'I promise you,' he said, 'I will never be a nuisance to you again. Just please don't hit me any more.'

Father: Well it looks like that ruffian has learned his lesson.

Cecil: Oh that's exactly what he said Fatherkins. 'You've certainly taught me a good lesson Cecil' he said, tears rolling down his cheeks and blood gushing from his nostrils.

Wilbur was absolutely furious when he entered the classroom. Things were not made any better when the first thing that Miss Stricto did when she had called the class to order was to make a beeline for his desk.

"And are you going to unlock the secret abodes of your sources and illumine us with the hidden light from your treasure troves of wisdom, Wilbur Barnes?" asked the stern-faced teacher.

"Yes, but not quite yet. Revealing my sources is just a tad more involved than referencing books and magazine articles, or downloading internet websites. Give me about a week, Miss Stricto."

"I'm not sure if my patience can last that long, Barnes. But if you want a week—this had better be good."

"Oh, it will be Miss Stricto, it will be."

At the end of the school day, Wilbur Barnes made straight for the same tree he had hid himself behind the previous day. He crossed over to the other side of the street and tied a piece of string around the tree directly opposite. He then ran back to the other side of the road and crouched behind the tree. Soon, he saw Smyth-Tomlinson and Fortheringay-Jenkins merrily peddling along the street. They were cycling side-by-side and joking and laughing as they rode along. Wilbur was quite sure that the cause of the merriment was the cock and bull story Smyth-Tomlinson had spun his father. Just at the right moment, Wilbur raised the string about a foot, and Smyth-Tomlinson and Fortheringay-Jenkins went clattering onto the road.

"How dare you, Barnes," hollered Smyth-Tomlinson.

"What is the meaning of this?" demanded Fortheringay-Jenkins.

"Oh Dadsie," said Wilbur mockingly imitating his foe, "I gave Wilbur Barnes such a hiding. I taught him a lesson. He begged for mercy—yack, yack, yack."

Wilbur's two foes were gobsmacked. They demanded of him as to how he could possibly have known of the conversation after he had left them.

Wilbur made no reply, he simply went over to the middle of the road, took the two bicycles and threw them into a nearby ditch. "Now start running," he commanded.

"Where to?" they asked.

"Anywhere. But I'm going to count to sixty and then I'm going to come after you."

"And then what?" asked Fortheringay-Jenkins."

"I'll run after you and catch up with you."

"But what will happen next?" asked Smyth-Tomlinson worriedly.

"Well," responded Wilbur ever so calmly, "I'm going to give you a hiding."

They ran as fast as their legs could carry them, but Wilbur did not come after them. He just doubled up in laughter at the sight of his enemies running in fright of him.

Instead of going straight home, Wilbur went off in a different direction. He walked along a tree-lined street until he came to a dome-shaped building. It was the town's planetarium.

"Come in, Wilbur," said the planetarium's curator greeting the boy. "What brings you here at this time? I'm afraid we haven't got any laser shows or celestial displays today."

"I need to have a talk with you, Dr. Loonar," replied Wilbur.

"All right, Wilbur. What can I do for you?"

"Dr. Loonar, could you send an invitation to my class to come to the planetarium for a show?"

"Eh, em, eh yyyesss," responded Dr. Loonar a trifle hesitatingly. "OK, I don't see a problem with that."

"Thanks, Dr. Loonar."

"If I may ask, Wilbur—why exactly do you want to invite the class to the planetarium?"

"Well, our teacher, Miss Stricto, asked each of us to complete an assignment on a subject of our own individual choice; I chose astronomy because I find it such an interesting topic," explained Wilbur.

"And you think that the shows which we put on here will help you with your assignment?"

"Oh, very much so, Dr. Loonar."

"But why can't you come to the regular sessions which we have here, Wilbur? And why your entire class?"

"It's like this, Dr. Loonar; Miss Stricto doesn't believe me when I tell her that most of my information is derived from my visits to the planetarium's laser shows and skymaster displays," lied Wilbur. Wilbur was not a boy who was wont to veer from the truth, but his overpowering conviction that any mention of Stellarman would be the cause of his being totally ridiculed and shown the door by the curator, seemed a reasonable enough justification for this little fib.

"Just give me about five minutes," said Dr. Loonar as he went over to his laptop. Wilbur waited while the curator tapped out something and then printed it out on a sheet of A4 size paper. "Now then, Wilbur, please give this to Miss Stricto."

Wilbur read the text Dr. Loonar had given him. His eyes widened and a big smile came across his face as he digested the contents.

"Than you Dr. Loonar. Thank you very much indeed."

"You are very welcome, Wilbur."

Miss Stricto snatched the piece of paper from Wilbur's hand and perused its contents. She said nothing as she folded the paper and placed it on her desk. She then looked hard at Wilbur as he stood before her in earnest hope of an affirmative response.

"No!" she blurted out. "We just can't have it. We are certainly not going to waste valuable class time by going to laser shows at the planetarium."

"Then I cannot possibly inform you of my sources," said Wilbur boldly.

"You'll reveal them boy whether or not we visit the planetarium. You'll reveal them simply because I tell you to do so."

"Miss Stricto. It is not a case of willingness or unwillingness, obedience or disobedience on my part with regard to the declaration of my sources, it is a question of what is and is not possible. If you spurn

Dr. Loonar's generous offer, I simply cannot (not 'will not,' Miss Stricto) enlighten you as to the nature of my sources."

Miss Stricto eyed her least favourite pupil all the more piercingly before she informed him that the final decision would rest with the headmaster. "Now, sit down, boy," she commanded in hot tempered tones.

"I just hope Mr. Dizplin will allow the class visit to the planetarium," Wilbur said to Stellarman that evening.

"Yes, I hope so too. Maybe he'll make his decision by tomorrow."

"The sooner the better," sighed Wilbur.

"We've concentrated so far on stars within the main sequence. Let's take a look at stars outside of the main sequence."

"When exactly is a star considered to have exited from the main sequence?"

"This happens when the star runs out of hydrogen at its core. However, the mass of a star determines when it leaves the main sequence. As stars burn up their supply of hydrogen, they increase in luminosity. When the hydrogen in the star's core is depleted, fusion ceases. The helium core then contracts; this results in gravitational energy giving way to thermal energy. There is still a shell of hydrogen around the star's core. The rise in temperature at the core heats this shell and hydrogen fusion starts and a greater degree of energy is produced."

"More than when it was a main sequence star?"

"Yes indeed."

"The increase in the radiation pressure results in the expansion of the outer layers of the star, this being necessary to maintain the pressure gradient. The expansion of the gas causes it to cool. By a convection process, energy is transferred from the shell to the star's outer layers thus increasing stellar luminosity by as much as a thousand."

"On which part of the HR diagram will the star then be located?"

"It will positioned upwards and rightwards from the main sequence line. This area is known as the Red Giant Branch—or, RGB for short."

"Is this what will happen to the Earth's sun?"

"Yes, stars of solar type will evolve to this part of the diagram."

"But I suppose then it will be different for other kinds of stars?"

"Yes. There is what we call the Horizontal Branch area of the diagram. HB stars have burning both in their helium core and outer shells. They move to the left of the diagram along its horizontal branch."

"What other branches are there, Stellarman?"

"There is the Asymptotic Giant Branch. When all the helium in the star's core has fused into carbon and oxygen, the core undergoes further contraction."

"So I suppose fusion into heavier elements starts at this stage."

"It depends. A star would have to be greater than eight solar masses in order to generate temperatures higher than 100 million K for this process to take place."

"What then happens to stars below eight solar masses?"

"Although no more fusion can take place, there is sufficient temperature to start helium fusion on the layers around the core. This in turn produces the heat to start hydrogen burning in the shell. These stars are located on the upper right area of the HR diagram."

"How much is known about the evolution of post-sequence stars, Stellarman?"

"It is very complicated and still not fully understood. One of the main things to note, Wilbur, is that stars off the main sequence do not live for very long."

"I suppose that that is why they are off the main-sequence."

"Yes. As we saw earlier, stars of very great mass burn up their hydrogen very quickly. In stars of five solar masses or higher, fusion of carbon and helium to synthesise oxygen takes place. However, as we just saw, stars greater than eight solar masses generate temperatures high enough to produce heavier elements in their cores."

Wilbur was very disappointed the following day when Miss Stricto said nothing about the possibility of a visit to the planetarium. However, his despondency was lifted not a little when Mr. Dizplin, the headmaster, walked into the classroom with a message for the pupils.

"Miss Stricto, children," began Mr. Dizplin, "I have just been on the phone with Dr. Loonar, the curator of the planetarium. He has invited this class to visit the planetarium tomorrow afternoon at one o'clock for a special show. A school-bus will be hired to take you all to and from the planetarium's premises. Miss Stricto, I hope that you and all the children will enjoy tomorrow's outing."

"Eh, Oh yes indeed Mr. Dizplin. I'm sure we are all very much looking forward to the event." Miss Stricto was doing everything in her power to both hide her annoyance and seem as enthusiastic as her acting abilities would allow.

Can you help Wilbur?

Find out as much as you can about the categories of stars covered by Stellarman on his latest journey with Wilbur.

What is a planetarium?

Have you ever been to one? If so, describe your visit.

XI

GALAXIES

The following day everyone alighted from the bus and filed into the planetarium's main entrance.

"Good afternoon everyone," said Dr. Loonar in cheerful fettle.

"Good afternoon, Dr. Loonar," responded the class in unison.

"We thank you very much indeed for this kind invitation," said Miss Stricto—again, trying as hard as possible not to show her true feelings. All of the pupils were glad to get a break from the normal humdrum routine of class work—only Cecil and Cedric appeared to be unhappy about the visit.

"Cecil?" said Cedric to his friend.

"Yes, Cedric," answered Cecil.

"I have a plan." Cedric Fortheringay-Jenkins then proceeded to whisper what he had in mind to Cecil Smyth-Tomlinson. "let's go to the back of the queue."

Miss Stricto kept a watch on the line of pupils marching into the planetarium. When everyone was inside the dark auditorium, Smyth-Tomlinson and Fortheringay-Jenkins sneaked out and tip-toed back along the corridor.

"That was a good idea you had Cedric," said Smyth-Tomlinson.

"I just don't see why we should be part of any arrangement which helps vindicate Wilbur Barnes," replied Fortheringay-Jenkins.

Inside the planetarium, Dr. Loonar asked everyone to be seated. "I'm so pleased to see you all today," he told everyone. "Now, first of all, we shall take a look at the constellations." Dr. Loonar then started the process of operating the Skymaster. He tried to put the display of the constellations on the domed ceiling overhead. A few minutes later, a somewhat worried expression came over the curator's face. "I can't understand it," he thought, "the Skymaster was working perfectly well only just this morning."

About minute later, a somewhat embarrassed Dr. Loonar addressed the assembled pupils. "Well, I'm eh, terribly sorry boys and girls," he said, his face going red, "we seem to be having a bit of a technical hitch with the Skymaster."

Expressions of disappointment invaded the faces of the children, only Wilbur showed no signs of emotion.

Suddenly a mysterious voice commanded everyone to be seated. "Will you all please sit down?" said the voice.

"Who is that?" asked Dr. Loonar.

"You will soon see who and what I am," responded the voice.

Miss Stricto rose from her chair and eyed the pupils intensely. "Someone is trying to be funny," she said, "and I think I know who our comedian is. Wilbur Barnes, have you got anything to do with this? Is this one of your stunts?"

"No, Miss Stricto," replied Wilbur with perfect calmness. "Now why don't you just sit down and enjoy the show of a lifetime."

"How dare you talk to me like that boy," snapped Miss Stricto. "I'll deal with you when we get back to the school." Wilbur just smiled a smile of contempt at Miss Stricto's threat.

"I'm afraid that there won't be any kind of show," lamented Dr. Loonar, "I can't get this machine to work."

"You won't need the Skymaster, Dr. Loonar," said Wilbur.

"Says who?" barked Miss Stricto.

"Says I," came a voice from the front of the auditorium. Everyone's breath was taken away when they focused their gaze on a strange icy-glass figure standing before the assembled spectators.

"Who on Earth are you?" demanded Dr. Loonar.

"First of all, Dr. Loonar, I'm not from Earth. My name is Stellarman and I live in the furthest reaches of the Universe. Hello, Wilbur," he said, smiling at the boy.

"Hi, Stellarman," said Wilbur greeting his friend.

"You, you know this eh em eh being?" queried Dr. Loonar.

"He is the source of my information. Dr. Loonar, Miss Stricto, classmates—please say hello to Stellarman."

Everyone gave an enthusiastic acclamation to the planetarium's mysterious visitor, only Dr. Loonar and Miss Stricto were a little hesitant in extending any signs of welcome.

"Are you having problems with the Skymaster, Dr. Loonar?" asked Stellarman.

"Oh yes," he replied shaking his head. "I don't suppose you can fix it?"

"I'm afraid not," was all that Stellarman replied.

All at once, a cacophony of disappointed 'aws' and 'hmmms' resounded throughout the auditorium.

"Well, children," began Stellarman, "since the Skymaster can't show us anything of the Universe, we'll just have to go around the Universe and see it for ourselves."

Everyone exchanged glances of great bewilderment with each other. Dr. Loonar asked Stellarman what exactly he meant.

"Well, I mean exactly what I say," Stellarman replied. "Now sit down everyone," commanded Stellarman.

When everyone was seated, there came a weird rumbling sound. This eventually gave way to a loud roaring; soon everyone was jolted by a most unexpected motion. The entire planetarium started to move upwards. Upwards and upwards it soared, higher and higher into the sky until it was beyond the Earth's gravity.

Terrified shrieks and screams emanated from the curator, teacher and pupils as they floated in a weightless gravity free environment. Stellarman attached a dial-type device to one of the walls and slowly started turning it. Gradually everyone started to feel weight returning to their bodies. After about one minute, normal gravity had returned and everything was back to normal again.

Smyth-Tomlinson and Fortheringay-Jenkins had also heard the rumbling and roaring sounds as they walked away in triumph from the planetarium's premises. Their feelings of self-satisfaction, however, were rudely stripped from them when, on their spinning round to see what all the commotion was about, they were at once filled with the utmost terror when they saw the entire planetarium taking off like a rocket. Up, up, up it went until it disappeared as a tiny dot beyond the clouds.

"What shall we do?" asked Smyth-Tomlinson.

"Come on," replied Fortheringay-Jenkins, "we must tell the police immediately."

"Well now, Wilbur," began Stellarman, "this is what we call 'artificial gravity.'" Stellarman was adjusting the instrument he had attached to the wall.

"Are we actually in space?" asked one of the pupils.

"Yes, we are; in fact we are now travelling through a time vortex. We can visit any place in the Universe in only a few minutes."

"Mr. Stellarman, sir, how can that be considering the cosmological distances between astronomical phenomena?" asked another pupil.

"It's because we Stellarmen know how to bend space and time and so create a time warp through which a space traveler can visit any place in the Universe he likes."

"Where are we going?" Miss Stricto asked.

"Wilbur!" replied Stellarman. "You choose where you would like to go; after all, it's for your project that we are making this trip."

"Stellarman! I would like to learn about galaxies."

"Alright—now does anyone know anything about galaxies?"

"A galaxy is an island of stars—billions and billions of stars," piped up one of the girls.

"That is absolutely correct," answered Stellarman. Now, Miss Stricto, do you know about the different types of galaxy?"

The teacher was still in a state of shock at what had just happened. She simply sat on her chair with her eyes wide open and motionless and blankly started at the wall in front of her. "I have no idea," was all she said.

"Until around the middle of the 1920's, there had been some debate as to whether what was generally termed 'nebulae' were part of our own galaxy or separate systems independent of it. It was the American astronomer, Edwin Hubble, who, using the 100 inch telescope on

Mount Wilson, confirmed that the 'nebulae' were in fact galaxies in their own right."

"And it was Edwin Hubble who classified the galaxies," said Dr. Loonar.

"Yes it was," replied Stellarman. In fact he identified three main types of galaxy—elliptical, spiral and irregular."

"I really don't care too much about galaxies," bleated Miss Stricto.

"Well, you're going to learn something about them whether you like it or not," said Wilbur. All the rest of the class started giggling, even Dr. Loonar found it hard to repress a bit of a chuckle.

"The first type of galaxy we shall look at is what is called an elliptical galaxy," said Stellarman.

"They are so called because their shape is generally ellipsoidal," said Dr. Loonar.

"Now look up at the ceiling everyone," said Stellarman. When everyone fixed their gaze upon the domed ceiling, they were treated to a spectacular display of a massive galaxy. This is Galaxy M87; it is in fact a supergiant elliptical galaxy. It is the dominant galaxy in the Virgo Cluster of galaxies."

"Are all elliptical galaxies so big, Stellarman?" Wilbur asked.

"Oh no! Not at all. Some contain only a few hundred million stars and some contain more than one trillion stars. And they vary in shape too—from being almost spherical to being very flat."

"It is also a characteristic of those galaxies that they contain mainly old stars of low mass," interposed Dr. Loonar. "As a result very little in the way of star formation is going on in these galaxies."

"Most astronomers concur that elliptical galaxies result from the merger of two similar size galaxies," explained Stellarman.

"What about spiral galaxies?" asked Wilbur.

"Hang on to your hats everyone," cried Stellarman jovially, "we are all going to take a trip to the famous Andromeda Galaxy. Would you all like to see this beautiful galaxy close up?"

"Ooooo yes please," said the children in unison. Only Miss Stricto was unhappy. She was still absolutely stunned and wasn't sure as to whether all of this was actually happening or whether she was just dreaming it. However, she was brought to her senses when, all of a sudden, the planetarium gave her a jolt as it gained warp speed and shot off towards the Andromeda Galaxy.

In just three or four minutes, the children saw the Andromeda Galaxy in all of its magnificence. They saw it as no-one had ever seen it before and as most likely no-one would ever see it again.

"A spiral galaxy has a flat rotating disk. At its centre it has a massive number of stars relatively close together. This stellar concentration is termed 'the bulge,'" said Stellarman after he gave everyone a few minutes to feast their eyes upon the glorious display on the ceiling. "They are called 'spirals' because of their spiral arms which go into the disk. These spiral arms are the cites of star formation and are thus brighter than the surrounding disk. Dr. Loonar, would you like to add anything to what I have said about spiral galaxies."

"Thank you, Stellarman. In fact, about two thirds of spirals have what is called a 'bar.' This extends from the bulge at the centre. Our own Milky Way is in fact a spiral galaxy and it has a bar just like most of the other spirals. Sixty per cent of all galaxies in the observable Universe are of the spiral type and are located in regions of low density. This means that they are hardly ever found in the centres of galaxy clusters."

"There is another fascinating feature that I should point out about the Andromeda Galaxy," said Stellarman. "It is that it is on a collision course with your galaxy."

Everyone shrieked with terror at the prospect of such a collision, but their fears were immediately assuaged when Stellarman assured them that this would not happen until another hundred million or so years had passed.

"Look," said Smyth-Tomlinson, "there is Constable Copper. Let's tell him what has just happened. The two truants rushed up to the policeman.

"'ello, ello, ello," said the constable, "an wot's goin' on 'ere. You two boys look a bit upset about something."

"Oh! Constable Copper, you're never going to believe what we are about to tell you," said Fortheringay-Jenkins.

"Try me," replied the policeman.

The two boys then told the policeman of the bizarre events at the planetarium.

"Let's go inside the station and tell Sergeant Bobby about it," suggested Constable Copper.

"Are you seriously trying to tell me that the planetarium simply just took off like a rocket and disappeared into space?" said the desk sergeant eyeing the two boys rather suspiciously.

"Yes," said Fortheringay-Jenkins, "that's exactly what happened."

"And why aren't you two boys at school?" asked the desk sergeant sternly.

"We had a school outing to the planetarium," Smyth-Tomlinson explained.

"So why aren't you inside the planetarium?"

"If we had stayed inside, we would have been whisked away into space," pleaded Smyth-Tomlinson.

"So you must have known it was going to take off then," the sergeant averred.

"Eh, em no," said Fortheringay-Jenkins.

"Then that leads me back to my question," continued the sergeant rather impatiently, "why did you two boys not go inside the planetarium."

"We did," Fortheringay-Jenkins answered.

"But as we got near the auditorium, we sensed that there was something wrong," said Smyth-Tomlinson.

"Hmmm," said the sergeant with cocked head, one eye closed and the other half-opened and through which he conveyed a contemptuous doubt at what had just been related to him, "I also sense that something is wrong."

"Now the third category of galaxy we are going to look at is what is termed 'irregular,'" said Stellarman. "They are neither elliptical nor spiral, and they have no bulge or spiral arms. They constitute around one quarter of all the galaxies in the known Universe."

"Will they become regular in the future?" asked one girl.

"No. In fact, they have evolved from being either spiral or elliptical. It is thought that extraordinarily strong gravitational forces bent them into their irregular shapes."

"Hubble identified two types of irregular galaxy," said Dr. Loonar. "The IRR-I galaxy types display some structure but not sufficient to definitively identify them as spiral or elliptical. The IRR-II galaxies are ones which are completely structureless."

"There is a third type of irregular galaxy which is called dwarf irregular," said Stellarman. "These are classified as DI. Their main characteristic is that they are metal scarce and gas abundant. This would seem to indicate that they are among the earliest galaxies as their stars have not yet synthesised the heavier elements. The study of these galaxies will greatly assist astronomers in coming to a better understanding of galaxy evolution and formation."

"I think we'll have to refer this matter to Special Branch," said Sergeant Bobby as he stood up and walked away from his desk and through a door located at the far end of the station. A few minutes later, he returned with two other police officers. "These are the two kids who claim that the planetarium took off like a rocket and whizzed off up into the sky."

"I'm Chief Constable Nick and this is Detective Inspector Clink," said the Chief Constable to the two boys.

"Your story, boys, is quite incredible," said Clink.

"Do you seriously expect us to believe it?" said Nick.

"But it's true," pleaded Fortheringay-Jenkins.

"We can't both imagine the same thing at the same time," reasoned Smyth-Tomlinson.

"No, but you can both play pranks at the same time," said Clink harshly.

"Why don't you go to the site of the planetarium and see for yourselves?" Smyth-Tomlinson suggested.

"The proof of the pudding is in the eating," interposed Fortheringay-Jenkins.

"Constable Slammer," said Detective-Inspector Clink to a police officer, "could you phone the parents of these two boys and ask them to come down to the station at once?"

"What else would you like to know about the Universe?" Stellarman asked Wilbur.

"Perhaps some of my classmates or Miss Stricto might like to suggest something," responded Wilbur generously.

One boy's hand immediately shot up. "Could you tell us something about quasars, please Stellarman?" the boy asked enthusiastically.

"Many people make the mistake of thinking that quasars are stars; in fact they are high energy regions at the centres of massive galaxies."

"Are they very distant objects?" Wilbur asked.

"They are indeed distant objects as they have a very large red shift. However, their red shift can also be due to the high energy output of these objects."

"Some quasars give off radio waves," explained Dr. Loonar. "This is because the electrons near their centre reach speeds near that of light. If there is a magnetic field nearby, the electrons will travel in helical paths and so emit radio waves. This is called synchrotron radiation."

"What exactly is their radiation output?" asked one girl.

"Some quasars are so luminous that they can reach radiation levels greater than those of ordinary galaxies. A quasar alone can generate the luminosity of two trillion stars. They radiate right across the spectrum from Xrays all the way to the infrared."

"Is it possible for amateur astronomers to see quasars?"

"No, not really. It needs large telescopes for quasars to be seen. When they were first discovered in the 1950's it was by means of radio telescopes. It was only after much searching that these strange objects of intense emission were detected by optical telescopes. With the advent of the Hubble Telescope, a lot has been added to our knowledge of quasars."

"What are pulsars?" asked one boy.

"These objects were discovered jointly by Jocelyn Bell Burnell and Professor Anthony Hewish in 1967. 'Pulsar' is actually short for 'pulsating star.' These stars emit regular beams of electromagnetic radiation."

"How does this happen, Stellarman?" Wilbur asked.

"It is because they are fast rotating neutron stars. Some emit their pulses in mere milliseconds while others do so in seconds."

"What are these mysterious objects known as black holes?" asked another pupil.

"This is a region of space/time where the forces of gravity are so strong that they prevent everything from escaping their grip. Even light itself cannot escape from a black hole."

"Can we travel forwards and backwards in time through black holes?" another pupil asked.

"These objects have been the source of many sci fi fantasies. In fact, they represent the end of the lives of massive sized stars. They normally form where there has been a supernova explosion. Once a supernova has blown most of its gas into space, the remains of the star has nothing to counteract the gravitational forces that remain. This results in the star collapsing in on itself. It does so to such an extent that it reaches the point of zero volume and infinite density thus creating what is known as a 'singularity.'"

"What is a singularity?" asked Wilbur.

"It is found at the centre of a black hole. It is where the curvature of space/time is maximal."

Can you help Wilbur?

Did you know that all the galaxies in the Universe are racing away from each other? Find out why this is.

How do galaxies form?

What do you know about 'dark matter?'

XII

TIME TO GO HOME

"I want to go home," bleated Miss Stricto.

"Oh! Don't be such a spoil-sport, Miss Stricto," said Stellarman. "The children are having a whale of a time."

"Are you enjoying yourselves, children?" asked Dr. Loonar.

Shouts of approval came from the whole class. Everyone wanted to see more and learn more of the mysterious Universe in which they were now traveling around.

"Before we do any more sightseeing," said Stellarman, "are you all a bit peckish?"

Everyone agreed that they would like something to eat. All the sightseeing had made them feel quite hungry.

"Would you all like a raspberry flavoured ice-cream?"

Shouts of "oh goody" and "yes please" resounded throughout the auditorium.

"Eh, I em er afraid," said Dr. Loonar in hushed tones, "that we don't have any kind of ice-cream here at the planetarium."

"I know that, Dr. Loonar," said Stellarman, "but I can make it for you if we change direction and set off for the centre of the Milky Way."

"What?!" exclaimed Dr. Loonar.

"Trust me," replied Stellarman.

By whatever weird and wonderful powers Stellarman possessed, he took the planetarium and its occupants straight to the centre of the Milky Way.

"Excuse me everyone for just one moment. I'm just popping outside—I need to activate my ice-cream making machine."

To everyone's utter astonishment, Stellarman disappeared from their sight. Wilbur walked over to Miss Stricto.

"Well, Miss Stricto," he began. "Do you believe me now?"

"I really have no choice, do I?"

"By the way, where are Cecil and Cedric?"

"Sitting somewhere in the auditorium, I would think."

"Oh no they aren't. I think they are truanting."

"Cecil and Cedric would never do that."

"Do you think so? Ask them to come here right now, please Miss Stricto?"

Miss Stricto got up and looked around the auditorium. "Cecil! Cedric!" she called out, but there was no response.

"I wonder where they are," said Wilbur.

"I'll get to the bottom of this when we get home," Miss Stricto said firmly.

Ten minutes later Stellarman returned carrying a large tray of raspberry flavoured ice-cream cones.

"How did you manage that?" asked Dr. Loonar in amazement.

"In the year 2009, began Stellarman," your astronomers discovered a substance called ethyl formate in a dense and hot region of Sagittarius B2. It is this substance which gives raspberries their flavour and has the smell of rum. By a complex process, it is possible to manufacture ice-cream from it. I'll explain more later, but meanwhile, let's all enjoy our ice-creams."

Wilbur and a few of his classmates helped Stellarman hand round the ice-cream cones.

"One for you, Miss Stricto," said Wilbur handing his teacher a cone. "Come along, Miss Stricto, slurp slurp." Wilbur was obviously making the most of the proverbial boot being on the other foot!

Everyone commented that this was the best ice-cream they had ever tasted. Dr. Loonar said that nothing on Earth compared to it.

"Let me continue now with what has been discovered by Earth's astrobiologists looking for tell-tale signs of life in space," said Stellarman. "If they can find amino acids in space, this greatly raises the chances of life's building blocks being a cosmic phenomena and planets being seeded from space."

"But Stellarman, you told us there are many civilisations throughout the Universe," said Wilbur.

"Yes, but the great question is—does life evolve in prebiotic soups in warm terrestrial ponds (and by 'terrestrial' I mean on individual planets) or are the building blocks an intrinsic part of the Universe's cosmic weave?"

"Have any amino acids been found?" asked Dr. Loonar.

"So far, none, but astrobiologists both on Earth and on other earths are engaged in the search for them."

"I thought that some highly advanced civilisation would have discovered them by now," commented Wilbur.

"On one particular planet circling a star in the Andromeda Galaxy, some scientists are developing a novel form of agriculture called 'space farming.' This is where I got the knowledge from on how to make ice-cream from space chemicals. Using the left-over whiffs of interstellar gas clouds that linger around their solar system, and bits of space debris like asteroids, meteors and such like, they are learning how to manufacture food in space from the abundant compounds which exist there. One aspect of this 'space farming' is the utilisation of barren moons and planets in their solar system. Both on Earth and on other earth type planets, people are asking about why the Creator made such planets which they see as hostile, barren and thus useless."

"Well, in the case of our solar system," said Dr. Loonar, "the giant planets, especially Jupiter, help stabalise the orbits of the Earth and the other smaller planets. They also act as 'vacuum cleaners' in that they attract, by their strong gravitational pull, asteroids and large meteors which, if they were to strike the Earth, would wipe out all forms of life on it."

"This is a general pattern that is found in many solar systems throughout the Universe," said Stellarman. "However, these large gaseous planets and smaller barren rocky ones, have other, as yet unknown, potentialities. The gas giants of this solar system in Andromeda are sources of energy for the inhabited planet. A couple of its watery moons have managed to evolve marine life. Massive robotic 'space trawlers' visit these moons and scoop up large quantities of fish which are then taken back to the inhabited planet. Large robotic manufacturing structures near the gas cloud remains, synthesise chemicals into many kinds of artificial foodstuffs—a kind of 'space soya bean' if you like. Glass domed structures on the rocky barren planets are home to agricultural and horticultural experiments. These complexes in space, around gas giants, and on rocky planets, provide means for the extension of food production and agricultural practices beyond their terrestrial confines. Scientists on this planet have now developed techniques for robotic mining. As their own terrestrial sources of metallic ores are now nearing depletion levels, they are turning to novel ways of winning metals from the moons, planets and asteroids of their solar system."

"And to think that some people argue that astronomy and space research are of no use!" sighed Dr. Loonar.

"Many scientific laws, such as those discovered by Newton and Einstein, were in fact discovered and confirmed through astronomy," said Stellarman.

"Many critics of astronomy and the space programme say that we should be concerned with solving the problems 'down here' before we start venturing 'up there,'" said Dr. Loonar.

"If we were to stand on the moon, then the moon is 'down here' and the Earth is 'up there,'" said Wilbur.

"Yes," replied Stellarman. "When we realise that the Earth is part of a much larger cosmic environment, then the distinction between what is 'up there' and 'down here' becomes somewhat blurred. And it is not only Earthlings who display this planetary parochialism, it is a common universal defect inherent in the mentalities of the peoples of many planets."

"Satellite technology has helped us in making more accurate weather forecasts and in monitoring the ecosystems of the Earth," explained Dr. Loonar. "And how could we operate our mobile phones and modern navigational systems without the aid of satellites?"

"And if the theories of Professors Hoyle and Wickramasinghe are finally vindicated, then medical science is going to have to widen its perspective in a cosmological direction in its quest to both understand the diseases which afflict mankind and unlock the secrets of their cures," continued Dr. Loonar.

"I have a question," piped up Miss Stricto.

It came as quite a shock to Wilbur that Miss Stricto would show any interest at all in the proceedings.

"Don't be too surprised," Stellarman whispered to him, "I put a generous lacing of rum in her ice-cream!" Wilbur did his best to stifle a giggle.

"I have a question," repeated Miss Stricto.

"Well then, Miss Stricto madam, and what is your question," said Stellarman in mocking tones.

"How can we justify the space programme when there is so much hunger on Earth?"

"Dr. Loonar, you know the Earth better than I do. Could you take on Miss Stricto's question?"

"Hunger is generally a transitory phenomenon," explained the curator. "It is caused by wars and natural disasters during which agriculture is disrupted and communication and transportation systems undergo breakdown. Other than that, no-one is starving—there is plenty food in the world. Many governments in what is known as 'the third world' use food supply as a political weapon whereby dictators cut off food stuffs to the opponents of their corrupt regimes. NASA and other space agencies cannot be held accountable for that. Another reason that can be cited for instances of food scarcity is the backward methods of agriculture in some countries. Because of inheritance laws that result in the constant division of land, modern mechanistic methods of farming necessary for increases in food production cannot be applied."

"Those who argue in this way," said Wilbur, "need to prove three essential points. First of all, they have to demonstrate a connection between the space programme and hunger—more precisely, they have to prove that hunger is a result of the space programme; secondly they have to convincingly argue that terminating the space programme would concomitantly terminate hunger; and thirdly, they ought to provide some precedent whereby the scrapping of a particular technology has had some beneficial effect on a social ill, be it hunger, homelessness or HIV AIDS!"

"Basically," said Dr. Loonar, "the critics of astronomy and the space programme need to furnish an example of how scientific and technological regress has ever given rise to economic and social progress."

"In fact," said Stellarman, "it is advancement in the sciences which have produced the spin-offs needed for improvements in the social welfare of mankind. This has been the case on every planet visited by not only me but by my fellow Stellarmen. Civilisations which have used the hunger argument as a pretext to scotch space programmes and other astronomical endeavours, have quite literally starved themselves out of existence."

"The case of that planet in the solar system in Andromeda that you mentioned, proves your point beyond all reasonable doubt," said Dr. Loonar.

"Indeed," replied Stellarman. "The governments of the nations on that planet have intelligently linked their agricultural policies to their space programmes. In fact, they are so successful that many farmers are now complaining of the low price of foodstuffs, due to an overabundance of them, driving down profits."

"It is 'the problems of success,' as Edward Heath (a one time prime minister) said of his own government."

"What about the burning issue of energy," asked one boy.

"Planets which have shunned nuclear energy and concentrated on a spurious 'green agenda' are the ones which have fared the worst in solving their energy problems," explained Stellarman. "Contrary to popular opinion, nuclear power is safe, clean and cheap. In fact the so-called green alternatives are among the worst polluters and not at all environmentally friendly"

"Has any civilization ever managed to achieve nuclear fusion?" asked Dr. Loonar.

"Yes," replied Stellarman. "The planet in that Andromeda solar system has achieved this feat in a unique way. They have built nuclear fusion reactors in space. Using the plentiful hydrogen available in space, they use a sophisticated form of gravitational collapse to create 'mini suns' inside these reactors. The energy produced is sent out in well directed intense beams towards energy relay stations on the planet. From there, it is distributed to both domestic and corporate customers."

"I hope this will happen on Earth one day," said Wilbur.

"I hope so too," agreed Dr. Loonar.

Can you help Wilbur?

What do you know about the idea of "terraforming" planets and moons?

Do you think that "space farming" is a realistic possibility? Why or why not?

Wilbur, Stellarman and Dr. Loonar are all of the opinion that the space programme and the science of astronomy are beneficial to mankind. Do you agree with their reasoning? Why or why not?

XIII

Down to Earth

"Ah, Mr. & Mrs. Smyth-Tomlinson and Mr. & Mrs. Fortheringay-Jenkins, do come in," said Chief Constable Nick to the respective parents of Cecil and Cedric. The policemen then related to them the boys' story of the missing planetarium.

"Well now," suggested Mr. Fortheringay-Jenkins, "I think we should go and take a look for ourselves."

It was agreed that they would all go to the site of the planetarium. Cecil and Cedric went in their parents' cars, and two police cars carrying Constable Copper, Sergeant Bobby, Detective Inspector Clink and Chief Constable Nick accompanied them to the planetarium.

"We will soon be home," Stellarman informed his group of space tourists. "I hope you have all enjoyed it."

Everyone was in total accord that it was the experience of a lifetime—well everyone except Miss Stricto. She had dozed off on her chair and was snoring profusely.

"Are there any questions you would like to ask before I take my final leave of you all?"

"Stellarman!" began Dr. Loonar, "I would like to ask you what many would consider to be a 'leading question' but one which I am sure so many people would be itching to ask you if they knew about you—does God exist, and if so what is the proof of His existence?"

"I have been asked that question time out of mind by rational creatures on myriads of inhabited planets throughout the cosmos. I can only reply to you in the same way as I have consistently replied to them which is that we Stellarmen, endowed as we are with vast capabilities, are not demi-gods, angels or other forms of superior being. We are fallible creatures who are born, live and die just like you. God is a matter of faith; just as some people believe in Him and others don't, so it is that Stellarmen and Stellarwomen develop their own specific philosophies and religious systems as to Who and What the Deity is. I personally believe in God, but that is my own choice, I cannot prove God's existence any more than any other finite creature can. I'm sorry to disappoint you, Dr. Loonar, but that is the only, yet honest answer I can give."

"May I ask you, Stellarman, how beings like you evolved separately and in so different a way from the flesh and blood creatures on planets?" Wilbur asked.

"We don't know our evolution any better than planet bound creatures know theirs," replied Stellarman. Many of our scientists and philosophers believe it has something to do with the underlying Intelligence that is inherent within the Universe. This Intelligence is created, like the Universe itself, so it is not God. So the generally accepted theory among Stellarpeople is that we are a sort of overspill of that Intelligence."

"But what about all that scientific knowledge which you possess?" asked Dr. Loonar.

"We gain our scientific knowledge from the inventions and discoveries made by scientists on the planets with advanced civilisations. As we gain knowledge from one advanced civilisation we take it to other civilisations which are advanced enough to benefit from it. For example, we can take television technology to planets which have already invented the radio, but not to planets which are still using animal power for locomotion. We suggest steam power to certain individuals of great intelligence and foresight who are living on worlds at this stage of technological progress. It was one of our number who inspired George Stephenson. That Stellarman learned about steam locomotion on a planet in the galaxy which your astronomers classify as M87. After studying your planet, he concluded that the political and social ingredients for an industrial revolution were in place in Great Britain, a nation located in the northern hemisphere."

"Amazing, Stellarman, absolutely amazing," exclaimed Wilbur.

"Well, boys and girls, we have landed. The planetarium is back on Earth. Although five hours have gone by here, only 30 minutes have gone by on your planet."

"Stellarman," said Wilbur with tears in his eyes, "will I ever see you again?"

"We Stellarmen and Stellarwomen have very busy schedules, we cannot stay long on any one planet."

"I understand," said Wilbur sadly. "Thank you, Stellarman, thank you for everything you have done for me. I only wish I could do something in return for you."

"There is something, Wilbur, there is. I want you to specialise in astrobiology and try and discover as many compounds in space as you possibly can. Then, I'm going to return and show you how to make and operate that ice-cream making machine. And then we'll work on advancing Earth's space farming technology; by then your planet should be in a technological state of readiness for it."

"I'll do everything I can, Stellarman, to bring the scientific community to a better understanding of the hidden biological nature of the Universe."

"That's the way, Wilbur. That's the way. Now let's go and waken up Miss Stricto. Stellarman and Wilbur walked over to Miss Stricto who was quite oblivious to the fact that the planetarium had landed. "Wakey wakey, Miss Stricto."

Miss Stricto struggled from her sleep yawning and bleary-eyed.

"That space galactic rum is fairly potent stuff, eh Miss Stricto?" joked Stellarman. Wilbur laughed through his tears. "I must go now Wilbur," said Stellarman turning to his friend.

"Goodbye, Stellarman, don't stay away too long," was Wilbur's parting words to his mysterious friend.

After Miss Stricto had doused her face with water, she ordered the class to stand in file and march out of the planetarium in orderly fashion.

As the pupils and their teacher exited the planetarium, the police had arrived with Cecil, Cedric and their parents.

"Well boys, your planetarium is still here," said the Chief Constable angrily.

"But, but . . . ." began the two boys.

"No 'buts' about it," said Detective Inspector Clink. "If you really must tell fibs, at least make your fibs credible."

Miss Stricto went over to the parents and police to find out what was going on.

"Oh! Miss Stricto," pleaded Cecil, "it's true isn't it, the planetarium took off and went up into space?"

"We told the police, but they wouldn't believe us," said Cedric.

Police and parents looked at Miss Stricto. Miss Stricto then looked back at them. Casting a glance of disapproval at the two boys, she said "Nonsense, it was all done by the latest version of Skymaster—all laser displays."

"I think, ladies and gentlemen," said the Chief Constable addressing Cecil's and Cedric's parents, "we will have to think about sending these two miscreants to an Approved School for a couple of months." With that, Cecil and Cedric were marched away by parents and police.

There was great excitement in the class the following day and Wilbur was the hero of the hour, not only because he was instrumental in bringing about the most amazing journey his classmates had ever experienced but also because he had got rid of the two most obnoxious pupils in the school. However, Wilbur was soon to find out that his joy would be short-lived. Miss Stricto wanted to see him privately in the staff-room.

"Now if you think that I am going to accept as valid references information that you got from tricks of light and shadows and this laser display called Stellarman, you are woefully mistaken," said Miss Stricto triumphantly.

"But Miss Stricto, you were with us when we went into space," reasoned Wilbur.

"Oh Wilbur, Wilbur. That was all special effects. My word, you do let your imagination get the better of you, don't you?!"

"But it's true, Miss Stricto."

"Go back to class, Wilbur."

Wilbur slouched back to class, hands in his pockets and head sunk low.

Later that day, the janitor came to the class and informed Miss Stricto that the headmaster would like to see Wilbur Barnes.

"What now?" thought Wilbur as he walked with the janitor to the headmaster's office.

"Ah, Wilbur, come in," said the headmaster.

"You wanted to see me, Mr. Dizplin," said Wilbur.

"I understand that Miss Stricto finds the references for your assignment untrustworthy."

Wilbur simply nodded.

"There is something in the video facility of your mobile phone I'd like you to show Miss Stricto," continued Mr. Dizplin. Wilbur whipped out his mobile. "Ah, don't look at it yet, Wilbur. Wait until you are outside my office. Look at it then, and afterwards show it to Miss Stricto. When you have shown it to her, come back and see me immediately."

Wilbur left the headmaster's office, took out his mobile phone and, curious to see what was on its video, activated the appropriate mechanisms. What he saw instantly cheered him up. He skipped along the corridor and into his class.

"Miss Stricto, could you please look at this?" said Wilbur grinning all over.

Miss Stricto looked at the monitor on the phone in Wilbur's arm, triumphantly outstretched before her face. She saw herself in the auditorium of the planetarium with a bottle of rum and a glass. There she was, swigging away, knocking back the rum as though it was going out of fashion—and slowly getting as—well, as is said in more vulgar parlance—'as pissed as a newt.' When the bottle of rum was finished, she saw herself keel over and crash out on the auditorium seat. Miss Stricto was absolutely stunned. She didn't know how to respond. Wilbur turned heel and left the class for the headmaster's office.

"Did you show your teacher the video?" asked Mr. Dizplin.

"Yes indeed. But may I ask sir, how did you know it was on my phone?"

"I'm leaving this school Wilbur. Tomorrow, a new headmaster will take over. I just wanted to help you before I take up my new post."

"Thank you sir," said Wilbur, still a bit puzzled by it all. He stood up and walked towards the door.

"Goodbye, Wilbur," said the headmaster.

As Wilbur turned round to say his farewell to the headmaster, he was absolutely astonished to find Stellarman sitting behind the desk.

"Stellarman. So, you are really Mr. Dizplin."

"No, Wilbur, Mr. Dizplin is really me."

Wilbur was completely overjoyed to see his old buddy again. He asked him about the magic he had used to change the images in the mobile phones and CCTV camera.

"Pre-technological civilisations which are abruptly introduced to aspects of science and technology way in advance of their state of technical development, tend to label as 'magic' the phenomena they have just been shown and as 'gods' those who display the gadgets to them. As I told you in the planetarium Wilbur, we Stellarmen are not gods. We are not omnipotent, omniscient or omnipresent."

"So how did you achieve those wonders?"

Stellarman gave out a good humoured laugh. "Your civilisation has a computer facility called 'photo-shop'—right?"

"Right," confirmed Wilbur.

"Well, to conjure up the images which were shown on the CCTV monitors and your mobile phone, I just used a much more advanced version of what you people call 'photo-shop.' A civilisation on a planet orbiting a star in the Pleiades cluster is now at this stage in its computer technology—this is where I learned about it. It involves taking a photograph of someone and superimposing it on a particular background. By various forms of manipulation, the subject can be made to appear to be doing all sorts of things—Cecil and Cedric dancing around in pink tights and getting beaten up by a girl, or Miss Stricto getting blootered on a bottle of rum. In a decade or so, your scientists will develop this technology. Nothing 'magic' about it at all, Wilbur. The scientists on the planet on which it was developed call in 'createvideo.' As I say, just a much more advanced version of photo-shop."

"Wow!" exclaimed Wilbur.

"Of course it's caused all sorts of legal problems on that planet; 'the camera cannot lie' doctrine has been completely demolished and video recordings can no longer serve as evidence in courts of law. No-one can be convicted on the basis of their crimes having been 'caught on camera.'"

"Can't their scientists distinguish between the real and the artificial?"

"It's something they're working on, Wilbur."

"And what about 'Mr. Dizplin?'"

"Nothing magical about that either, Wilbur. A planet in a distant galaxy has developed highly advanced nano-technology. Thousands of microscopic projectors strategically placed on a person or object can change the appearance of person or object by the mere press of a button." Stellarman then clicked at something behind his neck and immediately he became Mr. Dizplin. 'Mr. Dizplin' activated the same device in the same way and changed back into Stellarman. "One day, Wilbur, when you are well established in your career as a scientist, I'm going to return and teach you the intricacies of this technology. Together, we'll do so much to advance the human species as it exists on planet Earth." With that, Stellarman disappeared from his sight.

This time Wilbur danced back to his class with a joy he had never before felt, for now he understood that Stellarman would never be far from him.

What do you think?

Wilbur is very grateful to you for all the help you have given him. He now invites you to write about your ideas on how you think technology will develop in the future.

Do you think that the technology which Stellarman describes is feasible?

In what way will the computers of the future be different from the computers of today?

Will time travel always be confined to the realm of science fiction?

What about interstellar travel?